Magical Molly

& the Missing Treasure

by

Bolton Williams

MAPLE
PUBLISHERS

Magical Molly & the Missing Treasure

Author: Bolton Williams

Copyright © 2025 1ST (New Edition) Bolton Williams

First Published in 2025

Key Illustrator: Sharon Hinds

ISBN 978-1-83538-429-9 (Paperback)
    978-1-83538-430-5 (E-Book)

Book Cover Design and Layout by:
    White Magic Studios
    www.whitemagicstudios.co.uk

Published by:
    Maple Publishers
    Fairbourne Drive, Atterbury,
    Milton Keynes,
    MK10 9RG, UK
    www.maplepublishers.com

Magical Molly series

Book 1 – Magical Molly & the missing treasure.
Book 2 – Magical Molly & beginning of the end.
Book 3 – Magical Molly & the Phorceg Cup.
Book 4 – Magical Molly & the ultimate treasure.
Book 5 – Magical Molly & Paradise Island.
Book 6 – Magical Moly & the family's betrayal.
Book 7 – Magical Molly arrives in N. Ireland.
Book 8 – Magical Molly& the three Irish Kings
Book 9 – Magical Molly & Blue stack mountains.
Book 10 –Magical Molly & a family twist.
Book 11 – Magical Molly & the Cardiffians.
Book 12 – Magical Molly & the reading of the wills.
Book 13 – Magical Molly & the final encounter.

Pebble Powers and meanings

Slate pebble – News of utmost importance
Coal Pebble – Reasonable or strange news
Feather bound Pebble – Urgent reply required.
Orange Pebble – Long distance or abroad
Green Pebble – Castle messages
Glowing red Pebble – Imminent danger
Crystal, in silk pouch Pebble – No reply required.

Overhead chandelier and Miner's lantern

Colour coded translations
Orange – Tranquil/normal
Turquoise – Prepare for a spell.
Yellow – Wizard running late.
Red – Three feathers coach arriving.
White – Pebble arriving from goose.
Purple – Slate pebble imminent
Pink – Moonbeam descend.

CONTENTS

Chapter One

The battle at Symonds Yat

The battle at dawn was ending; the two families of the kingdom had been fighting for what they each believed was theirs. The final gong sounded as the Crogg family from St. Clears retreated, their tall hats dishevelled on their bald heads as they reluctantly acknowledged that they had lost. Although they had caused mayhem, they had fewer members left standing. Thus, Owain Glyndwr, Head of the Welsh family of Wales, and owner of the "Welsh Wizard Weekly" periodical had declared the competition won by the Llewellyn family.

Tudor Llewellyn, moving quickly despite being injured, had grabbed the treasure chest, one of the three contested treasures, checked the inside for the rare Hugglett love spoon, and slammed the lid shut. He caught Ivor's eye from a distance, and they exchanged a brotherly message. Tudor went ahead with urgency towards the oval glass coach, where he would be flown back to his castle, with two of the treasures, safe in the hands of the Llewellyn family.

Ivor, even though equally injured, was rounding up his closest allies as his warriors saw to the dead and wounded. An immense amount of dead and wounded even though they had won. Elijas lay on the ground as

Ivor bent to check if he was alive. There was no point trying to use his magic, it was diminishing. After three hours fighting, he could not remember any spells. Ivor could hardly get up as he checked Elijas for a pulse and as he looked around for his other companions, Geraintus came puffing up to him, his breath as green as his giant frame.

"Garibaldi is unable to walk Ivor. Use the golden coracle to transport both Elijas here and Garibaldi. I can pull them back to the coach."

"That's kind of you Geraintus, where is he, is he alright?"

"He is frightened; the last spear caught his long beard and brought him to the ground. If he'd been of wizard proportions and not a dwarf, it would have killed him Ivor. None of our spells are working anymore; we're all too exhausted. At least we've won; we are the first family of Wales.

"It doesn't feel like it Geraintus," said Ivor getting up gingerly from the side of Elijas who was in a poor condition.

"He's alive, we need to get him home to administer a few potions and let's hurry. I don't trust the Croggs; they may come back and counter attack."

Bedivere came into Ivor's view, dragging a shaking dwarf with the look of death on his face. His eyes swollen and his floor-length beard torn in places, making it look like an unevenly knitted jumper.

"Geraintus, get the coracle and put Elijas and Garibaldi in it. I know you're a giant, but can you manage to pull it, we need to get to the coach. Tudor is already striding ahead, but he'll wait for us."

Ivor, with Bedivere, his trusted friend by his side wearily walked towards the glass coach which had been hiding, to collect the wizard family. Geraintus, the green giant, robes torn and chunks of flesh weeping from his massive torso pulled the remaining treasure which had Elijas and Garibaldi, Ivor's servant, and dwarf, placed inside.

"Did Tudor check the treasure chest for the paperwork, authenticating the love spoon to the coracle, Ivor?"

"Yes, we have it. I'm too old for this nonsense Bedivere; we can at least relax now in our kingdom and truly claim all those castles as ours."

"I know the crest of the Crogg family is close to ours Ivor, but we are the rightful owners of this treasure. Surely, Owain wouldn't have allowed a group of three-foot carpenters wearing tall hats to run the kingdom?"

"Strange as it seems, Owain is sometimes too fair for his own good, he only thinks of his reputation, which is a great one. We must remain fair to the people; we owe them that. Trust me, the treasure was always ours. I can tell you another day, Bedivere."

"You obviously have something to share with us, Ivor...."

"What the devil is that?"

Without advance warning, a gang of armed and hooded warriors surrounded the wizards as Ivor quickly threw his flamboyant cloak over the coracle hiding Elijas and Garibaldi. But more importantly, covering the remaining treasure from being spotted.

Bedivere at an equally grand old age as Ivor, of a hundred and forty-two years, responded as quickly and started calling out spells to stop the spears from hitting them.

"Benialli, benalli," they both shouted and repeated as they had no spears or arrows.

"Geraintus go ahead and check on Tudor, he isn't to be seen, we'll deal with this lot," ordered Ivor sounding more confident than he felt.

The heavily armed soldiers spoke rapidly, throwing spears at the wizards and the coracle. Missing Ivor by inches, both Ivor and Bedivere continued to chant spells, the spears responding by returning to the sender, confusing the warriors. As they retreated, Geraintus came puffing back from the side road, his green skin even darker, splattered mostly with new blood, as his giant frame had been like a wall, the spears bouncing off him.

"Tudors disappeared along with the treasure chest," he panted, blood pouring from his cheek as he whispered a spell which stopped the bleeding.

"Goodness me, has he gone by coach, or has he been kidnapped?" queried Ivor. He desperately wanted to sit in the coracle himself but knowing they'd saved it by covering it with their cloaks, he couldn't very well just give up. He checked Elijas and Garibaldi again, they were both out of it, but alive.

"No idea, Ivor. The glass coach is hovering over the oak tree; we're minutes from it we'll have to pebble him to find out once we get inside."

"Hurry then," Bedivere commanded, out of breath and positively shaking with the mere fact that the last lot of spears had tested their resolve. They needed to source someone who could help strengthen their magical capabilities. He cast this notion aside as he helped Ivor and Geraintus move the coracle to the steps, now dangling out of the coach which had whirled towards them.

The oval coach came to a halt, its spindly claws grabbing the ground for balance. The slipper glass steps hovered in the morning breeze as Ivor checked Elijas and Garibaldi once again, covered the coracle with his silver and blue moon cloak and murmured another spell,

"Velez Rubio/Veles-Roobi-oh."

The doors slid open, and the coracle rose in the air, moved up over the steps and flew inside the coach. Geraintus, Bedivere and Ivor, head of the immediate family followed. He checked over his broad shoulders, for enemies, soldiers, or Tudor even. There was no sign of anyone; the warriors had disappeared as quickly as they'd sprung upon them.

"Vamos, adref/ Vah-mos Ah-drev."

Garibaldi was asleep and Elijas was in a coma. Bedivere started attending to them as Ivor and Geraintus repaired his torso and cloaks. Ivor's wounds were superficial as he had a thick skin and had spelled invisible armour on his body ahead of that morning's contest. He wasn't going to allow a bunch of carpenters get the better of him. He sighed as the coach whirled softly above the hedgerows, flying from Symonds Yat to a cave in Saundersfoot, Ivor's headquarters.

Ivor watched the dashboard of the coach, and then he realised that he'd forgotten the password to change the route if he needed it. That was the final straw; he knew that he must summon Magical Molly to assist. He'd suggest this to his comrades once they'd returned and had checked if Tudor were indeed kidnapped or alive at any rate. If this was the case, the family had a problem, and they needed help. More to the point had the treasure chest been stolen from the very hands that had saved it.

The dials within the dashboard of the coach winked as if in response to Ivor's thoughts. The three communication feathers on the roof, twitched, as if knitting a scarf while talking to itself.

"Shall I get the pebble sack out for you, Ivor? Bedivere's busy with Elijas and Garibaldi so we might as well send out messages whilst we're travelling,"

suggested Geraintus, who realised Ivor seemed to be pre-occupied.

"Yes, yes Geraintus. I have a plan, that's all."

The pebble sack was always on the shelf above the coach dashboard, within reach to whoever was driving the ship. Thankfully for Ivor he'd registered the instructions in the memory box much earlier. Ivor knew that help was needed as a matter of urgency for at this moment he couldn't remember any spells.

"Find the most important pebble of all, Geraintus. We need to ask Kester; Tudors bat if he's dead or alive."

"Which one is it, I always forget the colour codes of these things?" said Geraintus going greener than usual with slight embarrassment.

"Don't worry Geraintus, I've a list on the back of my front door to help me remember, or Gari does it for me," chuckled Ivor giving himself a few extra seconds' thinking time...

"Send the feather - bound one, Geraint," whispered Garibaldi from the coracle and promptly went back to sleep.

"Yes, he's right. Kester will need to respond to it immediately, it would be useful to know that Tudor is safe before we get home."

Geraintus quilled a message back to front and placed the pebble in its own pouch, then flung it through the communication exit muttering the postal spell the family used when sending pebbles,

Ivor Llewellyn- Head of the First Family of Wales.

"Boh-st ee-boh-st," repeating three times.

"Send the next one to Merlin as a matter of extreme urgency, we need Molly at once," said Ivor as Geraintus scribbled furiously.

"Why Ivor?" exclaimed Bedivere rising from his kneeling position as he finished administering potions to Elijas and Garibaldi. He came and sat next to Ivor as Geraintus finished writing.

"Bedivere, something's happened to Tudor. We, therefore, must assume we've lost the treasure chest and, as you're very aware; our Hugglett spoon was inside it. Without the spoon, the coracle will not function, nor will they be able to cast the spell on us, and so to continue to make us superior to the rest of the kingdom. I only hope the parchment inside the treasure chest hasn't been taken, to registering the treasure as ours. We need to file the paperwork at the town hall, to make the announcement official in the Welsh Wizard Weekly that we've kept the title of "First Family of Wales."

"Where's this pebble being sent Ivor? It's ready."

"Merlin is in Spain, send it to him there. He will summon Molly over by moonbeam at first light tomorrow."

"What if Tudor is okay and the chest is with him?" asked Bedivere.

Plop.

"From Slobbers. We'll know right away," said Geraintus as he picked up a slate pebble from the dash of the coach.

Geraintus went a paler green than usual as he read Slobbers' message.

"What is it?" said Ivor anxiously.

"Tudor attacked, in a coma, treasure chest missing. Arrive through secret passage spelled in readiness."

"Slobbers, efficient as usual"

"Tudor wasn't attacked by the Croggs Ivor, they were much bigger and taller," said Geraintus trying to work out whom they'd been.

"I've no idea, who they were either. They spoke Welsh but I couldn't grasp what they were saying as I was too busy, as was Bedivere, protecting the coracle and of course Elijas and Gari."

"Send a pebble back to Slobbers, Geraintus. Inform him that Molly will be arriving tomorrow and that we'll need to make room for Elijas to recover along with Garibaldi. Make sure he understands that his master is more shocked than injured."

Geraintus completed the messages and sent them through the feathered exit as Ivor and Bedivere sat together, making plans for their next move. The treasure had been stolen from them. However, they had the golden coracle but they both knew that without the spoon the coracle was useless. They, as a family, needed the treasures together to install the spell they needed to keep them magical and powerful.

"We'll worry about who tried to attack us, once we get home, Ivor. I'd concentrate on preparing some

magical lessons for Molly. I hope you've warned Slobbers, Garibaldi even. After all Ivor, Garibaldi's cat has his own powers."

"Yes, yes, Bedivere, I know what you are implying, but Garibaldi and I have already spoken last week regarding Magical Molly. He'll be okay about it, leave Slobbers to me."

The coach started to shudder as it descended and disappeared from the outside world as it shrank into the dunes of the beach of Saundersfoot, where Ivor's cave was nestled into the skyline, sand in colour and quite hidden from the average naked eye.

"Datrys ar unwaith/Dah treece ah een-waheeth," murmured Ivor several times as the coach doors opened and the coracle slid out, the steps acting as a slide.

"Gari!"

"It's okay Slobbers, he's in shock, he'll be fine. Help us get them into their beds and then we need to plan what we do next. We've a problem," reminded Bedivere.

The glass coach twitched, clicked its three feathers communication system, and excused itself away from the living room through the back passage until it was needed again. Geraintus with Bedivere helping, placed Elijas in a hammock in the parlour and Garibaldi, was placed on the coracle couch, his fragile condition needing the warmth of the fire that Slobbers had lit earlier.

Slobbers, thankful that he was still the top cat, was even more grateful that his master was alive and not in a coma. Kester had messaged him much earlier than the Wizards; he could see that their spells were diminishing as Garibaldi had told him in confidence. It was now very apparent that they needed to locate the lost treasure, but what was this about a top dog? He made the Aloe Vera special brew and took the teapot into the dining room, where the two wizards and Geraintus were discussing their imminent problem.

Slobbers poured tea into three large mugs and returned to the kitchen to find the chocolate biscuits, Bedivere's favourite and Welsh cakes which Garibaldi had made fresh that morning, prior to the battle.

"We cannot wait for Tudor to recover and ask him, Bedivere," said Ivor, a bit agitated with him. *"Tudor may be the eldest, but I'm still head of the family. I am the one living in a magical cave with rights to live in most of the castles. Tudor may already be living in Caernarvon Castle, but he was given that as an inheritance. I can reside with my comrades in all the castles that are empty. Having the treasure, gives the Llewellyn family the right to live in these castles, I surely don't need to remind you, Bedivere?"*

"Ivor, our problem is that we've lost the spoon and the parchment in the treasure chest. Bedivere is only trying to remind you how urgent this is," whispered Geraintus as he raised his giant eyebrow at Slobbers, who shook his long black and silver striped tail in acknowledgement.

"Is there something you're not sharing with us, Ivor?" quizzed Bedivere sipping his tea.

"No, no, no it can wait. The most important thing now is to prepare for Molly and hope Garibaldi recovers to help us organise her imminent arrival party," said Ivor.

"In the meantime, Ivor, I'll go and check out a few of the creatures in the neighbourhood and report back later. Whoever took the chest will still need the coracle. They might not know that but surely, we need to hide the coracle just in case someone decides to come looking for it," said Geraintus, needing to return to his own home. The family would need extra support with Elijas out of it and now Tudor seemingly in a coma too.

"Geraintus is right Ivor. I'll leave too. I'll see if I can shed some light on who attacked Tudor. This will give you time to organise some lessons for the dog, bring her up to speed with our spell system and our coded lanterns and family protocols. Geraintus, no one can register the treasure unless they have it all. I suggest we keep the coracle hidden or spelled until we can regroup tomorrow."

Ivor closed the door on his two friends. He was very weary indeed. He made his way to the couch and sat near his friend and dwarf servant, who'd been loyal to him for over a century. Garibaldi knew Ivor had made a mess of things in his life. However, he wasn't going to allow his past to affect the rights that his family had earned. His past had nothing to do with recovering the treasure and Molly would help them.

She was the most magical creature that had been born unto the Llewellyn family of late. Her skills and intuitive gifts were needed at once. Tudor would have the treasure returned before he came round from his coma, Ivor was convinced. It was only a matter of tactical thinking and logical planning with Bedivere, and they'd soon locate the whereabouts of the chest that housed the spoon.

Chapter 2

Magical Molly's imminent arrival

Morning came quickly and a weary Ivor awoke to Garibaldi humming around the cave, working his magic, and attending to Elijas.

"Gari, how are you feeling? You took quite a battering, are you sure you're all, right?"

"Yes, eat, Elijah has stirred too. Our ability to recover using our magical potions hasn't left us yet, Ivor. I know about Molly arriving at sunrise, I've asked Hattie to organise the welcome party, and all the invited guests have been notified."

"You've been busy, Gari. Have you explained to Slobbers why we need Molly?"

"Yes, he knows she's the first magical dog born to a Llewellyn with unique qualities needed to find the spoon. They'll get on fine, Ivor, they'll need each other."

"Where is he?"

"On errands for tonight's party."

"I need to prepare some lessons for Molly and re-arrange the cave ready for her. Have you received news about Tudor?"

"Yes, Tudor is recovering, he may even make tonight's event, and Kester seems to think we might see him this afternoon."

"My that's a quick recovery from a severe attack."

"Uhm my thoughts exactly. Why don't you sort out the cave, whilst I see to Elijas and prepare the "**hovel."** Molly will need to know what this is, and I need to get it ready."

"We've so much to tell her before she has hope of helping us to locate the treasure. Gari where is the coracle. We need to keep an eye on it."

"It's not magical without the spoon Ivor; it's outside on the beach. You can see it from the kitchen window. I've cast a Hugglett spoon spell on it. It will be safe there. No one will be able to come this close to the cave while Slobbers is patrolling the beach. We're the only family that knows its special powers when the spoon is attached to the coracle's link chain."

"Yes, you're right. I need to start on my lessons. I'll see you later."

Garibaldi collected his basket and adjusting his baggy red and orange striped jumper, showing signs of fraying at the edges, made his way to the front door. He checked the pebble list on the door serving as a reminder to Ivor, who kept forgetting which pebble was needed for message sending. He also glanced at the lantern on an oval table in the hallway. This along with other artefacts in the cave gave the wizards advance warnings of trouble brewing or other happenings in the community. This was significant in maintaining the authority which the wizards would soon lose if the spoon weren't found quickly. The lantern would fill with coloured smoke, to indicate whatever was going on. The list of the colour codes hung on the back of the door, along with the pebble communication list.

Garibaldi sighed. He wasn't stupid and knew this was going to be a dangerous treasure hunt. They'd been attacked twice yesterday. Someone else had an interest in finding the spoon, not just the Croggs. Elijas had been murmuring the same worry in his troubled sleep as Gari had been attending to him. He left Ivor writing at his bureau. Gari had enough to think about, and he would talk to Slobbers later. They needed to bring Molly up to speed with the goings- on as soon as she arrived.

Ivor scribbled back- to- front at his bureau, his peacock feather quill moving effortlessly on the parchment. He stopped for a moment and realised; he didn't have a clue how to prepare a lesson plan for Molly.

Rat-Tat-Tat

"Goodness that was loud!"

Ivor held the dripping quill upside down as he opened the front door and gasped as Tudor stood there, in his burnt orange cape glowing with little red dragons, making him look every inch a wizard of importance. His six- foot square frame towered over Ivor, who stepped aside for him to enter. He was agitated and carrying a package.

"Tudor that was a remarkable recovery, even for you. Whatever happened?" said Ivor placing his quill back in its pot. Shuffling his papers together; he didn't really want Tudor to know that he was struggling with Molly's lesson plan, if indeed she needed one.

"Ivor, I knew you didn't think I'd been attacked, but that's up to you," said Tudor, very agitated.

"Let me make some aloe Vera tea, you look like you need some, Tudor. Gari is out, so let me put the kettle on. Sit, won't you?"

Tudor spun his cape over himself as he settled into the coracle couch and picked up the latest issue of the Welsh Wizard Weekly as he waited for Ivor.

Ivor, in the kitchen attending to a dozen or so Welsh cakes on the slate platter, could sense something was amiss with his brother. He was annoyed that Molly was coming so soon and staying with him and not with Tudor at Caernarvon Castle.

He brought in the cakes and tea and checked his lantern to be sure and indeed it was a tranquil orange, which meant everything was normal. The crystal chandelier above them also housed orange-coloured thimbles at each tip, a confirmation that all was well. His other benchmark was his very own shepherd's stick with a curved hook, the thimble on the end, also orange. With all his checks in place he sat at the table and Tudor joined him. Immediately, Tudor uncovered the package he'd been carrying. It was a replica lantern to Ivor's. Ivor noticed that his hands were shaking.

"You have something to tell me, Tudor. Were you attacked and what's this lantern full of shredded parchment?" asked Ivor determined not to let his brother outwit him.

Tudor grabbed a Welsh cake and sighed.

"Look I know you don't believe me Ivor, but I was attacked, those warriors were like giants and there was a dozen of them. They took the treasure chest and when I came to; I found this near my torn cloak.

"Kester told us you were in a coma," said Ivor agitated with Tudor.

"I couldn't trust anyone. I got to the castle, I had been roughed up, that's all. I found this. Someone left it by mistake when they took the chest."

"I see," said Ivor not convinced.

"I noticed," said Tudor as he started to rush his words. The truth dust in the Welsh cakes beginning to take effect as Ivor smiled, and waited.

"The Welsh Wizard Weekly mentions we have coracles being repaired in the Swansea area, if anyone needs any. Why do you think the Croggs of St. Clears are building new ones, Ivor?"

"How do you know that Tudor?" Ivor stopped smiling. This was not good news.

"*Kester my bat; has been hanging around in various ill-reputed bars in St. Clears trying to gather information on who attacked me, but no news as yet apart from this coracle business.*"

"*Tudor, Molly will be here this sunrise. I know you don't want me to train her, but the decision is made. She will stay here; we must all be one family if we're going to claim the right to live in the empty castles which are ours. As you know, we need the treasure registered before we can declare we are the first family. Surely faking your capture and losing the treasure chest isn't exactly brotherly support, is it?*"

Ivor had said too much, Tudor got up, his face as red as a tomato. The Welsh cakes had taken effect. He waved his hand towards the lantern, the torn parchments inside started to bounce with the power of the breeze behind Tudors' agitated hand.

"*I **am** on our side Ivor, believe me. The Croggs have started training that Beggly army, we have trouble afoot. I'll return through the passageway. I'll send Kester to meet Molly on my behalf. Sort these papers Ivor; they may be a clue to where the treasure chest is. I shall be at my castle when you realise that I'm on your side. We need to forget our differences if we're to reclaim ownership of those castles.*"

Before Tudor could organise a spell to get back to his castle via the passageway, his body decided to let off an incredible amount of wind and he was propelled headfirst through the passage before Ivor could wave farewell.

"Thank goodness for Gari. That truth dust does work! I must ask him to get some more," chuckled Ivor as he got up to move Tudor's lantern next to his own.

It was time to check his cave. Elijas walked through from the parlour but looked a little fragile. Ivor smiled at him,

"Are you recovered enough to get to the Inn, Elijas?"

"Yes, Ivor, I'll make my way there now. Whatever was in that awful smelly potion Garibaldi gave me worked indeed, thank you."

"Tudor's been here, we can discuss his surprise meeting when we're all together later Elijas. Bedivere and Geraintus will be there already, I shall be following you in due course."

"Righto Ivor," as Elijas closed the front door quietly.

Ivor picked up the red collar which had been hanging over the hook near the lists all this time. Studded with turquoise stones it was a collar to be worn by the most magical member of the Llewellyn family and Ivor hoped that was Molly. He was relying on it. The collar's significance might help Molly find Ivor's treasure as well as the family's treasure.

Garibaldi knew everything, and surely Garibaldi would advise him if he felt he should come clean. He couldn't face his brother or his best friend Bedivere with his past. He couldn't bring himself to even think about it, how ashamed he felt.

Now, it would have to wait. Finding the treasure chest and the Hugglett spoon was far more important than his seedy tale involving only him.

They needed to get to the Red Dragon Inn as Molly was due any time. The front door opened as Slobbers and Garibaldi piled in with a mountain of brown bags of groceries and packages. Slobbers took them into the kitchen as Garibaldi adjusted his jumper, yet again.

"Everything is in order, Ivor. The people of the parish are expecting us, Slobbers is going to St. Clears to spy on the Croggs, as we need to know why they've called a meeting at their town hall. I received a message earlier. What's this other lantern?"

*"I'll explain when we get to the Pub, Gari. We need to leave; I shall change into my most mystical cloak. Send Slobbers with a pebble so he can send us a message. Prepare a **double- pin** to his collar I don't trust anyone right now, Tudor's been here, need I say any more."*

Ivor went to change as Garibaldi and Slobbers arranged a **double - pin** on his collar. Slobbers, who had a thick silver coat, put a small pouch under his grand belly as Garibaldi placed pebbles inside.

"Don't be stupid Slobbers' and don't swim just because you're able. Be back as soon as you can. Molly will need a top cat beside her, and you're aware of all the family secrets as I am. Be safe, Slobb," as Garibaldi hugged him, passing on his unique powers to his beloved cat. Slobbers mission to spy on the Croggs would look good when Molly started asking questions about the other

family. Information, he hoped that should lead them to the stolen treasure chest. Even he was flabbergasted as who had attacked Tudor, let alone Slobbers who had spies everywhere.

Ivor returned as Garibaldi closed the door on Slobbers.

"Where's the red collar Ivor?" asked Garibaldi as it was missing from the back door.

"It's in her quarters, Gari. She should wear it as soon as she gets here. Shall we go, the cave is secure. Did you open the **hovel** *in readiness?"*

"Yes, we're done Ivor. The golden coracle is on the beach. It will not be taken as it's heavily spelled for anyone to get near it."

"Who is patrolling the beach in Slobbers absence?"

"Geraintus has sent a few owls from his kingdom. Once Slobbers returns, they will fly back to his patch. It's all in hand Ivor, let's go and wait for Molly. The sooner she helps us, the better," reassured Garibaldi knowing deep down this family, his family, were indeed in a pickle. Even Ivor himself didn't realise how grand a pickle.

❖

Chapter 3

The Croggs of St. Clears.

"**Q**uiet *quiet everyone.* Can I please have some order?" shouted Kentav Crogg, as the congregation ignored him. He stood on the platform, behind the table with official looking parchments placed in piles. The audience continued chattering as Trent got up from his chair and slammed his stick three times on the table for maximum effect. The noise subsided and all eyes turned towards Kentav Crogg.

"At last, I'll begin."

Kentav was the eldest of four brothers in the Crogg Family of carpenters. He wore the tallest Welsh hat as he was the eldest, making him tower over everyone, which was the purpose of being in charge. The hats were two feet tall and the average Crogg appeared five feet high with their hats on in public. These hats were as black as coal and had a broad rim, used as a shelf when the Carpenters were working in their factory.

Most of the Croggs sported round freckled faces. They had bald heads save for a tuft of orange hair on the forehead. This was why they wore Welsh hats in public. All these faces looked up at Kentav. He knew there was unrest as they'd lost the battle for the treasure and everyone in the room was convinced that the treasure should have been theirs. Kentav cleared his throat and placed his pipe on the slate ashtray on the table. He leant on his own stick as he explained,

"We're building new coracles to take the coracle which Ivor Ap Llewellyn has hidden at his cave house. Ali here will summarise where we are to date and then I shall continue to tell you, our plan."

Ali stood up and got straight down to business.

"We've made fifteen coracles and need more volunteers to help us. We've stored the ones we've built already at our tea shop in Laugharne. They'll not be noticed there amongst the boats in the boathouse."

"Why do we need to build coracles?" someone from the audience shouted out.

"Good question. We're going to steal the golden coracle from Ivor's cave, as it's on view on their beach. We need to row through the waterways in coracles, capture the golden one and take it to our hiding place, right away. Once we've captured the coracle, we'll start searching intently for the treasure chest and the Hugglett spoon. We will conquer and get those castles. They're ours," shouted Ali, getting quite animated.

A Beggly jumped onto the wooden table as the audience cowered and moved back slightly. The whole room went quiet as this creature hadn't been seen before.

"This is Zupp, head of our Beggly army. He has spied on the Llewellyn's in Saundersfoot for over a week, which is why we know the golden coracle is at Ivor's beach. We're going to need more help to build coracles. Can we have hands for volunteers please?"

Some hands went up as Blodwen, Kentav's wife made notes of who was going to help in her book.

In the meantime, the creature jumped from the table and disappeared as instantly as he'd arrived. He had spotted something in the audience. He wasn't a spy for no reason.

Kentav got up as Blodwen continued to print the names of Croggs, who were going to be paid overtime for helping to make coracles.

"We're going to need as much cooperation from you all as possible; thank you."

"How many more coracles, do you think we need to carry out the mission?" asked a member of the audience.

"We need ten more. We already have fifteen, that should be enough but the sooner we get them done; the sooner we can attempt to take the golden coracle from Ivor's beach. The spy has done a decent job, we must work fast. I'm asking the volunteers to work on Saturday as well as the Sabbath."

Blodwen sat down having written seven new volunteers on her paper. Kentav continued to talk, as he liked the sound of his own voice.

"We shall have a meeting again next week. Can you all stay off the ale and stop chattering in the pubs as walls have ears. We must keep this a secret. Anyone found talking in public, will be hung, and beheaded by the Begglys. They don't take any nonsense. As you all know, Ali here has trained them all to kill."

"Shall we tell them where we are going with the stolen coracle," whispered Trent but not quietly enough. All the three- foot Croggs in the first few rows overheard and started to stomp their feet, shouting,

"Tell us, tell us!"

Kentav annoyed with Trent (and not for the first time that day) got up quickly and hit his pipe on the table for silence,

"We cannot risk telling anyone of the planned route or where we will hide the coracle just in case someone lets it slip. You must trust me no one wants a secret like that as they would be beheaded if the Begglys are told who leaked the information. See you all next week."

All heads in the room nodded in silence and agreement as they hadn't liked the look of the Beggly even though the creature was meant to be on their side.

Trent knew he'd wound his brother up again, by not sticking to the script. Everyone shuffled out of the hall. Some of the excited Croggs went across to the Pig and Crest pub and the rest went home. Kentav arrived at his semi- hutlet, which had been purposely built to look down on the other hutlets on the common. Most of the hutlets belonged to his family, with Trent, and Ali, a little way down from his. Petre, the fourth brother, had been banished from the community for courting a Llewellyn; how much the hatred was amongst the two families. The charred remains of his hutlet burnt to the ground were a powerful reminder to everyone that Kentav Crogg was ruthless.

Blodwen was already making supper as Kentav arrived with his two brothers at his heels. Jethro and Bethesda joined them at a long table and Kentav beckoned everyone to sit. Trent, knowing he was in trouble again, declined and lit his pipe and sat by the fire. One of Kentav's' seven daughters helped Blodwen serve the men and then departed afterwards, leaving them to talk.

Jethro was the local undertaker who supplied all the wooden caskets for the dead. He sported one green eye and one black eye. He was disliked as he buried little people. Bethesda was the local minister for the parish and lived in the house next to the chapel. They all sat drinking tea as Kentav started talking.

"It won't be long before we're ready to take the coracle."

"These Begglys, are they ready? We need more of them; we should have slaughtered the Llewellyn's at that battle Kentav, what happened?" Jethro questioned, his black eye making Kentav slightly uncomfortable for a moment.

"The wizards are more magical, than we thought. We know they're losing their powers, but we didn't

estimate they had their warriors with them. Owain's army, even though he'd declared a battle. You must realise we're up against the First Family of Wales, but we will be that family soon, I'm determined. Are you all with me? It's time to reclaim what's rightfully ours."

Kentav lit his pipe and everyone else followed suit, the blue smoke drifting over their heads as the conversation continued.

"We don't have that chest. I have no idea who took it. Tudor was ambushed on the way back to the castle, but at least we know that the wizards don't have the spoon either."

"Have you heard that Magical Molly is arriving at sunrise to help them?" said Bethesda.

"Why the interest in the dog that's arriving Bethesda, what's your point?" asked Trent from the chair by the fire.

"Well, I'm aware her grandparents are in Talley, by the lakes. We need to be placing spies everywhere that involves her. She'll visit her original family, I'm sure. It's just a suggestion Trent."

"Good point Bethesda. Ali, send a Beggly there tomorrow. Currently, we're on schedule to take the coracle next week, it will coincide with the family settling down the dog, which should distract them."

"How are we going to take the coracles over to Saundersfoot, without being noticed? Those wizards have spies everywhere?" asked Trent.

"We'll use the waterways; hide the coracles in the mass graves that the Begglys have been digging out these last three weeks. They cannot be seen unless you know they're there. Not even that big cat Slobbers has noticed, and he patrols the beaches daily. We're ahead of them. We shall conquer those idiots very quickly and be living in Cardiff Castle or any castle you fancy, before we know it," Kentav beamed and even more as his wife of thirty years, walked into the room with more tea in her large teapot.

"I still want to know why you think the Llewellyn's haven't got the spoon, Kentav. What makes you think that the coracle on the beach is the golden one. If it were that important, surely the family would have it hidden under lock and key somewhere."

"Ali has a point Kentav," chipped in Bethesda.

"I can assure you all, that they haven't got the spoon, my spies are that trusted. Would you argue with one of your own home - grown Beggly Ali?"

Ail shook his head, as he knew he had reared a deadly species and that they sometimes got out of control. Even he had some doubts about managing them at times.

"We need someone to go to Caernarvon Castle as Tudor "was ambushed" apparently and he may have the parchments that were in the chest. We need to send someone to search his castle."

"I could go in the capacity of Minister. We need to organise the next local talent competition and there's *been talk that Tudor would open the castle to the public for the event. That's as good excuse as any to see him quite quickly,"* suggested Bethesda.

"Excellent idea, go right away. We shall convene next week after the meeting at the town hall to plan the day of attack. Good night," as Kentav dismissed them with a wave of his freckly arm.

Trent muttered good night as Ali and he left the hutlet to walk down to their respective huts further down the hill. Ali stopped and nodded at Trent as he went inside his own. He lived alone; having been jilted at the altar, he would never look at a Crogg again.

Trent nodded and walked to his own hut, glad it was Friday tomorrow as he would be taking a coach to see his girlfriend, a half Llewellyn. This was a complete secret and the last person he wanted to know of this was Kentav, as he would blow a gasket. Fraternizing with the enemy, he would be banished from the Crogg community. Petre's charred hut was evidence of what could happen to him if Kentav found out.

Kentav lay in bed with his Blodwen and smiled knowing they had an active Beggly army multiplying as the creatures did, daily. They had no spells or magical powers, but they had plenty of volunteers to fight. He wasn't daunted by challenging the Llewellyn family. On the contrary, Kentav Crogg was determined to live in Castell Coch, his favourite one of all. He was going to prove to all the Crogg community that Kentav was the first Crogg in the entire history of the family to live in a castle.

***

Somewhere in Tregaron, the same day, a family had been given a treasure chest, near to Symonds Yat, whilst on a picnic. They hadn't looked inside the chest yet and it sat in the hallway of their temporary home, undisturbed.

A Romani family had been given the chest as the warriors had witnessed them being attacked by bandits. They had rescued them, helped them on their way and had given them the chest, having first rummaged through but finding nothing of value or worth keeping.

Deep inside the chest, a slate spoon started to wriggle out of its silk pouch. It was trying to contact the golden coracle.

Chapter 4

The Llewellyn plan commences.

"*Ivor, over here,*" beckoned Bedivere as Ivor's allies sat together on the terrace as the party was in full swing.

"*She was collected on time via our coach,*" summarised Geraintus shifting his giant frame in the garden chair as Ivor walked over and looked perturbed.

"*Ivor, you look troubled what's wrong?*" asked Bedivere sensing Ivor's worries.

"*Tudor wasn't attacked as we thought; but he did lose the chest, which is a huge blow to us. He left a glass lantern with torn papers in it. Tudor believes the attackers left it by mistake,*" said Ivor.

"*Where's the lantern now?*" asked Elijas his hands still shaking from his ordeal.

Ivor not answering Elijas continued,

"*Tudors mentioned the Croggs are making coracles and we've an abundance going cheap and yet they're building new.*"

"*That need's investigating right away,*" said Bedivere knowing Ivor's powers were dwindling faster than he'd previously admitted.

"Garibaldi is on it; he's already sent Slobbers in advance of Molly arriving. We need to be ready for action the minute she's able to help us."

Before any discussions could take place a smaller dwarf than Garibaldi ran through each room shouting,

"She's here, she's coming...she's coming......."

"Garibaldi will have a feast for us at home once we've done introductions. Please come in order we can plan a strategy right away," said Ivor getting up. The whole party along with invited creatures and wizards of the community went outside to welcome the glass coach.

From a distance the crowd could about see the glimmering oval shape of the coach skimming the hedgerows. The three gold and silver feathers that functioned as the radar could be seen twitching as the coach came closer. The spindly legs started to unravel, and the claws grabbed the loose gravel on the ground as it came to a halt.

There was silence around the coach as it spluttered and coughed. With great force the glass steps flew out of its belly and glided to the ground quietly. The door slid open, and Molly stood in awe at her reception. A ball of fur plopped down the steps and rolled to a stop as everyone looked on mesmerised, as Molly came down with the ball of fur under her.

"Welcome Molly," said Ivor going forward as everyone cheered. The glass steps disappeared, and the

coach whirled itself away from the waiting contingent leaving a pile of luggage strewn against the pub wall.

"*Hello Ivor,*" said Molly turning her paw to shake his hand. "*Meet Yo-Yo who's a bit shy. I hope you don't mind him being here with us. He's highly intelligent and he attends to my collars and cloaks.*

"*Of course not,*" said Ivor as Molly nuzzled the ball of fur. Yo-Yo unravelled himself to stand next to her barely reaching her tail tip.

Yo-Yo was a sausage type dog who was chocolate brown in colour, and he wore a studded black collar. The collar which looked far too big for his tiny frame generated a force even Ivor acknowledged as he shook his paw. Molly had arrived with more support than was requested. Ivor guessed she was more intuitive than he'd imagined which excited him suddenly.

The gaggle of geese organised by Hattie started playing the traditional harp tunes as Bedivere suggested they all went into the pub for Molly to meet the locals. Hattie, also acting as head waiter was already moving round the pub with slates of baby frogs and snails with a few of her colleagues.

Molly and Yo-Yo received a bowl of special water as they sat with Garibaldi who was introducing the wizards to her. Molly looked round as she knew the harp was dispensing a spell to ward off the enemy. She hoped she would live up to the family's expectations of her.

Immediately Yo-Yo was running round the place getting in and out of the way of the waiters and making friends very quickly; for which Molly was grateful.

Molly, a Border collie was just two years old and first born to the magical Empire and the Llewellyn family. She'd shown immense powers and magical abilities from an early age and the decision to help the wizards had not been entirely hers. She had her own personal reasons for helping Ivor Ap Llewellyn to find his treasure. Molly realised as the pub started to empty, that her own treasure was equally precious as these missing treasures. She hoped that she'd have the same help for when she shared her very own personal missing treasure.

Yo- Yo had already gone ahead with four square suitcases on his back as Ivor, Bedivere, Elijas and Geraintus walked with Molly back to the cave. Yo- Yo barged through the door toppling Garibaldi as he rushed through and dumped the luggage on Molly's bed. Garibaldi, mouth open just looked at Ivor who smiled.

Garibaldi ushered everyone into the dining room, where Tudor sat on the couch to everyone's surprise, especially Ivor.

"*Why* Tudor I thought you were sending Kester to say hello?

"I wanted to meet the Magical Molly myself," said Tudor getting up from the couch, shook paws with

Molly immediately as Garibaldi insisted, they all sat at the table.

"Hi, you're Ivor's brother Tudor. I've been briefed. Where's Slobbers, Garibaldi? Will he object to two dogs arriving and not one?"

"He'll be fine and will be pleased to meet you both, I'm sure of it," said Gari as he placed welsh cakes and chocolate biscuits on the table praying Slobbers wouldn't feel left out.

"Do you use the passages to move around from Castle to cave?" asked Molly wanting to get on with building information as quickly as possible.

"Yes, we've three tunnels in effect, one goes to Tudors, the second is used by the three feathers coach and we keep the third for our own private use. This enables us as a family to keep ahead of everyone. We must maintain the powers that we have. The tunnels currently are keeping the community from knowing that our spell function is waning."

"I think we need to discuss what we know to date and then start immediately on tackling the problem," suggested Molly taking a welsh cake from the slate plate.

"Yes of course," said Ivor clearing his throat to start the story.

HISS- HISS- HISS- HISS…….

*"Goodness, it's the **hovel**, something's wrong," declared Garibaldi as he rushed to the parlour to see.*

BARK- BARK- BARK

"It's Yo-Yo he's in the herb garden Ivor."

Molly rushed into the garden followed by Bedivere and Elijas as Tudor held back, his bat already there. Yo-Yo was barking at the sunflowers which held Kester hanging and this mayhem continued for a moment as Molly's purple collar started to tingle round her neck.

CRASH- CRASH –CRASH

"Ivor," called Garibaldi rushing out to the garden. *"Whatever's going on as our lantern is curling blue smoke into the hallway and that other lantern, which Tudor brought, has crashed to the floor and those pieces of paper are flying everywhere?*

"Goodness me what's going on?"

"Yo-Yo dig under the sunflowers," instructed Molly as she realised that Kester was trying to tell them something.

Garibaldi went with him and as Yo-Yo dug, he found something.

"Look a transmitter, we're being bugged?"

"Tudor do you know anything about this?" asked Ivor going quite pale as it dawned on him that his treasure hunt was going to be more complicated than he'd envisaged.

*"**No** Ivor. I **object** to you believing that I'm the enemy. Kester come; we're going home. Kester bought this to your attention Ivor. If he weren't on your side,*

he'd have left the transmitter there. Get a grip, we're not the enemy. Good day Molly, we'll see you another time," stated Tudor his annoyance with Ivor clearly showing through his red cheeks. He spun his cape around him and strode deliberately towards the passageways and left.

"Re- do the flowers Yo-Yo but check the rest of the flowerbeds and let's all see this Hovel. Why is it screeching and what exactly is its function, Gari?

Molly eager to find out why the cave was in chaos suddenly needed to know why her collar was also getting tighter round her neck.

Inside the cave, Geraintus with his notebook and quill confirmed the cave was on lock down. Everyone went to see the hovel as the blue smoke in the cave subsided. Elijas was clearing up the papers and had successfully used a spell to repair the lantern, which he now placed on the dining room table.

Inside the parlour on a square wooden table sat the hovel. It resembled a white porcelain sink and was a foot-deep inside. It was activated by a family spell and housed several double pins around its perimeter. These double pins were attached to animals and wizards and could be tracked on the hovel. It would also hiss if enemy factions were close to any family member and warn the Llewellyn's in advance.

"An example of it working is here Molly. See this double pin, it's Slobbers; he's on his way home from St. Clears. Why he's on this route we can't say, but he'll be

able to tell us when he gets home. He should be here tomorrow. However, this purple-coloured dot shows movement in Tregaron."

"Why Tregaron?"

"That's a good question Molly, we're not sure but something's moving in Tregaron relevant to us."

"Someone has the treasure chest and it's in Tregaron. We need to act. I must tell you that my collar's tingling around my neck, something's happening Ivor."

"Spell the hovel to hiss even louder if this purple dot moves again Gari. We need to know if the collar responds to this movement."

Everyone returned to the dining room as Elijas had started to look through the torn papers.

"Where did these come from Elijas?" asked Molly as she witnessed that Yo-Yo was following Garibaldi round the cave learning all his spells.

"The enemy supposedly left this lantern of torn papers, when they attacked Tudor."

"Is there anything of interest on them?"

"Look, what have you got in your mouth?" asked Ivor taking a torn piece of paper from Yo-Yo, as he jumped and did cartwheels, pleased Ivor had seen what he'd found under the table.

"It's got letters on it, a double LL, what does that signify?" asked Molly.

"It could mean Castell which is Welsh for castle. Elijas, spread them all out this could tell us something," said Bedivere as he got up to join Elijas at the far end of the table.

"Ivor, explain to Molly the family history and I'll make some tea. The sooner she's up to speed on the past, the quicker we can try and find the spoon," said Garibaldi feeling quite sick. This treasure hunt was more than just finding a spoon, his gut was giving him that same feeling that he'd had the last time the family had a dreadful disaster.

"I also need to visit my grandparents at Talley lakes as I believe there may be a message there for me with the lady of the lake."

"Well yes Molly, we didn't realise you were so thoroughly informed. Shall I brief you on the family problem and then we can plan our search," said Ivor who realised that Molly didn't need lessons, although he would suggest she had a few with Garibaldi to check she was this clever.

Garibaldi ahead of Ivor as he should be as his loyal servant, chipped in as he placed another teapot on the table, *"We've a lesson planned in a moment Molly, on the beach. Once you've been briefed, we'll move the Golden Coracle. I've secured your spell on the coracle for it to recognise you,"*

"Well done, Gari. I look forward to your lesson. Ivor, tell me the story whilst these wizards are getting on with this puzzle of papers."

"Owain Glyndwr, who is fighting the English, declared a few months ago that treasure had been found. He claimed it belonged to us the Llewellyn family. Our name derives from the Hugglett love spoon, which is the only slate spoon ever made. This spoon was given to Ivor's ancestors as a gift declaring him and his family, the First Family of Wales. The spoon acts as a key to open any castle in Wales, of which we own and can live at our discretion.

This love spoon was made to be attached to the Golden Coracle which is on the beach. The link chain and the Hugglett spoon will create the powers and spells. Together they cast a spell on us as wizards and we continue to live for another fifty years. The treasure chest which has golden emblems of our crest carved on it, one crest is a candle and candle holder, along with parchments inside confirming this.

One day Owain wrote in the "Welsh Wizard Weekly" that some treasure had been found. We needed to officially declare it was ours, which we did, and we had to wait forty days for it not to be contested. On day thirty-nine, the Crogg family from St. Clears, declared the crest resembled theirs and declared an interest therefore a battle.

Reluctantly, Owain agreed a contest had to be actioned as he's a fair man. Yesterday we lost the treasure after having won it. We were attacked leaving the battle with the Coracle and the chest. Tudor had grabbed the chest, trying to be helpful and he in turn was attacked. You know the rest we have the coracle and no proof *it's ours. We won the battle, we are the first family but someone out there, thinks otherwise. We're not entirely sure, if it's the Croggs or if there's someone else trying to take our Castles from us, which is what this is all about really."*

Before anyone could make comment, the lantern in the hallway started curling blue smoke again. The thimbles in the chandelier overhead began to jangle and the sublime ambience of the room changed, chilling everyone as suddenly there was more barking from Yo-Yo.

"IT'S MOVING. LOOK IT'S MOVING."

Garibaldi and Molly jumped out of their chairs quickly followed by Geraintus and Ivor. The lantern continued to turn turquoise blue, and then dark blue as Bedivere and Elijas tried to concentrate on the paper puzzle.

Yo-Yo curled into a ball and went ahead of Garibaldi to investigate as the gate opened from the other side and slapped Yo-Yo head on.

SMACK! This resulted in him being flung through the air towards the sand dunes. There, stood on the path was an exhausted and injured Slobbers.

"Slobb you're hurt. We're going to check on the coracle, what's happened to you?" said Garibaldi.

"Go and check on the coracle Gari. I'll fix Slobbers and join you in minute," said Molly who wanted to show someone her magical attributes. She needed to feel as smart as these wizards for some reason.

Slobbers' paw was dripping blood and hanging off by its claw. He had lumps of fur missing from his bulky frame. His faintly striped tail appeared broken, and he was lame.

"Let me fix your tail, before it goes white and then we'll need a vet, we can't have that," whispered Molly as Slobbers stood wobbling on three paws. Molly started her spell.

She stood erect her bushy tail upright and grabbed his tail, she turned round three times repeating her spell, her tail throwing silver dust over his as he spun,

"Benilioni cyweiriad/ Ben-ee-leonee Cuh-weh-rheead."

Slobbers came to a standstill as Molly's brown glass eyes glazed over which made Slobbers fear her for a second.

"Lay on your side Slobbers, I need to fix the paw."

Slobbers followed instructions, he was in capable hands, he could see.

"Sagra, gwaaeyd/gwah-ayed," she repeated three more times swishing her tail and sprinkling dust from her tail again.

The paw repaired itself in front of Slobbers' eyes and he was convinced. He'd had his doubts but no more. He knew deep down from his conversations with Garibaldi that this family owned all this treasure but were far from able to locate the missing spoon without help.

"I'm sure you've loads to tell us, but let's go and investigate the coracle first. Yo-Yo, who you hit with the gate unknowingly is in the dunes somewhere," smiled Molly.

"Goodness, is the coracle moving?"

"Yes, let's go."

"Gari, what's happening?"

"Mollys fixed you then. The coracles' twitching, it's trying to prise itself away from the pole that I placed here for its security."

"Why?"

"Slobbers, I've no idea. Molly, stay away from it, as it might pick up, you're here and make it even more agitated. I've no idea, what to suggest."

"It's wet inside too Gari look," said Geraintus who was as confused as everyone else.

"Where's Ivor?"

"Looking for Yo-Yo, he's prodding all the dunes with his shepherd's stick. I don't know why he doesn't spell Yo-Yo back here."

"That's precisely why we've a problem, he may not remember Gari."

"Let's look at the coracle, what should we do?"

"Overa tah-eeth," repeated Molly swishing her tail as Yo-Yo in a fur ball could be seen flying towards them as he landed on his four feet directly looking into Slobbers' face. He quickly went under Molly as he realised that this was Slobbers, and he was as magical as he.

"Hi sorry about the gate," said Slobbers rolling his tail round his little tail as they bonded immediately.

Ivor came over knowing his spells were at a crucial stage and needed an influx of power from these treasures soon, as he looked at Garibaldi who nodded and understood.

"Why is it wet?" said Ivor also.

Inside the Golden Coracle was a double seat made from ash, with family emblems adorning it. On the seat there were several markings, one looked like an indentation for a key, and another looked like a saucer, waiting for its goblet. There was a paw indentation. The very bottom of the coracle had silver moons and stars emblazed over it. To the side of the seat edge was a link chain, which appeared to have a few links missing. The oar which was attached to the seat also had stars and moon symbols on its tip showing part of the green candle, the Llewellyn crest.

"This all depicts our family symbols Molly. It's impossible to believe this coracle belongs to anyone but us."

As soon as Ivor spoke the coracle turned to its left, then right, rose three inches in the air and shuddered before returning to the sand. It started to wriggle as if trying to get away from the pole. It rose again, turning right and tried to unhinge itself, as everyone stood back. As this was happening, Molly's collar began to tingle yet again as she yelped.

All the family went to her aid, but before then she turned three times, her bushy black and white tail erect in the air and with her glass eyes, threw a spell at the coracle, not waiting for Ivor's permission,

"Beh-van-aly, greeg-oall-ah," she repeated.

The coracle moved again, turned right and left and then sighed, its oars clapping each other, resting on the seat as if it had given up.

"The bottom's dry Ivor" said Geraintus as he peered closer.

"I'm not convinced that this coracle is safe out here. I know it's close to the cave and when Slobbers isn't here, we have Geraintus owls, flying about. We need more help to protect ourselves Ivor. This coracle needs to be inside secure within our cave and not just within our sights."

"It is Molly it's tightly spelled by you actually and we can see it from every porthole in the cave."

"Ok, let's go inside and find out what Slobbers has to say and then we must make plans for me to visit my relations at once. The sooner we find out what's going on the better," said Molly thinking that the security around the place seemed very lax.

Her purple collar was tingling again, and Ivor assumed she needed to wear the red collar. This was the simplest solution yet; but he hadn't suggested it. Too much was happening too quickly. The sooner they understood from Slobbers what he may have seen, the earlier she could leave and visit her relations. The lady of the lake would have some information for Molly to find the missing treasure. He hoped.

Chapter 5

Molly practises some spells.

Slobbers sat at the top of the table as Garibaldi prepared more tea as the others sat around to listen. Yo-Yo was following Garibaldi everywhere; he knew everything he needed to know about the cave and its workings. He'd even memorised all the spell systems from the back door and knew how and what each pebble meant already. He knew this was of utmost importance for Molly if he was to continue to be her aide. He wondered if Slobbers would be happy.

Slobbers, who felt important right now started to explain his mission and why he'd got injured.

"I arrived at the town hall in St. Clears a bit late as the meeting had started. It was packed with Croggs, and they were very noisy. I had to hide which was a bit difficult, but I wanted to get close to the front as I couldn't hear Kentav say everything. They're building new coracles to steal ours, simply put."

"I knew it, we must move the coracle right away Ivor," said Bedivere horrified.

"Yes, let's hear it all first," said Ivor going quite pale but agreeing with Bedivere.

"They don't have the Hugglett love spoon, and they presume we don't have it either. They've had one

creature called the Beggly, spying on us for over a week Ivor. I imagine someone is spying on us right now."

There was silence round the room, as Geraintus got up to find out if his owls were still in place. Slobbers would normally be patrolling the beach.

"Anything else Slobbers?" asked Molly, who needed to sort the security immediately as otherwise the coracle would be gone from under their noses.

"They're making more coracles; they've about ten more to build. Once they're ready they intend to come through the river system to take the coracle. They're hiding them in the tea shop in Laugharne. I was so angry with the Beggly for spying, I left the hall to follow him, and I jumped him. I nearly got killed," sighed Slobbers shuddering.

"Well done, Slobbers, did you kill him?" asked Yo-Yo who jumped on Geraintus' lap to hear the rest of the story.

"I jumped him, but his antenna sent a shock wave through me, sending me flying. I landed on a chimney top, which broke my tail. I fell off the roof and saw him go across the road. I followed him. He threw me again, with another spark. The shock went through my body as I flew into someone's coal house, landing in the bunker. I couldn't move for a day and the little old lady who came in that night with her bucket for coal would have had a fit, if I'd been a different colour.

The next morning, I overheard the men talking from the factory workshop. They were going to Laugharne, and I managed to crawl inside their truck. They've all the coracles stored there, for when they're coming to get ours. On my way home, I noticed there are mounds of moss craters around the riverbanks. We must investigate what they are as they weren't there a few weeks ago. It's the Beggly army, they're deadly. We've a problem," said Slobbers quietly.

"You're indeed a Top Cat Slobbers. Are you willing to help me, and Yo-Yo retrieve the treasures for this family?" asked Molly anxious for the air to be cleared having heard his story of how organised the enemy seemed.

"Yes of course Molly. We need to act fast."

"I do believe you need to move the coracle inside the tunnel Ivor. I can use that same spell to help you move her right away. In the meantime, I'll have that lesson Gari if you think I need one. We need to finish that paper puzzle wizards and Ivor; you must prepare for us to leave for Talley at once. Can you summon the coach? We must act now."

"Bedivere, Geraintus, you're all magical, sweep the cave and ensure we're not bugged. Gari and I will be back shortly. I suggest Slobbers and Yo-Yo start patrolling outside with Geraintus' owls, we're more vulnerable than we thought."

The lantern on the hallway turned white in colour as Yo-Yo looked bewildered as he knew this meant a pebble was arriving, it was all very spooky.

YELP -YELP

The purple collar around Molly's neck started to agitate her again as Ivor rushed to look as the goose knocked on the door.

"Pebble for Ivor," he cackled and waddled away.

"Bedivere, Garibaldi the collar round Molly's neck is getting tighter have a look while I read this pebble," said Ivor. *"It's slate, it's important."*

Bedivere and Garibaldi could see Molly's eyes were glazing over and suddenly Ivor was going pale in his coracle chair. The lantern Tudor had brought suddenly crashed to the floor again. The second lantern started curling out purple smoke once the white smoke had subsided, this was a rare occurrence.

"Ivor what's in that message, it's affecting our lantern, it's apparently quite key to our mission," said Geraintus. *"Take Molly's collar from her neck she obviously shouldn't be wearing a purple collar."*

"Geraintus is right, take it off. Look at her she's rolling her eyes, this isn't good at all," said Garibaldi.

The collar was taken off Molly's neck as Ivor continued to mutter, *"Goodness me."*

"Ivor for goodness' sake, what is it, can you at least share it as it's affecting Molly, something isn't right," said Bedivere.

"Moh-llees, moh-llees thau," muttered Elijas as the glass lantern repaired itself and everyone turned their

heads to Ivor even Molly was back to normal, Yo-Yo by her side.

"*You read it Gari,*" sighed Ivor as he passed the parchment inside the pebble to Garibaldi.

"*My Cousin Ivor,*

Once I left you victorious in your quest for the Hugglett spoon and treasure chest, I was sorry to learn that you were ambushed near Symonds Yat and lost your treasure. That same day, I witnessed your brother under attack on his way, I presume to Caernarvon. Being the local wizard, I intervened in the battle. I realised that Tudor was unfairly beating a much smaller warrior to a near pulp, who had no strength to steal his chest. I took the chest away from Tudor not realising at the time that it was yours to keep.

In Tregaron, I saw a Romani family about to be tortured to death and the little boy was already strewn upon the kidnapper's horse. I rescued the family and gave them your treasure chest innocently thinking there must be at least some gold coins and clothes inside, to help them on their way.

Your last pebble confirms that this happened in Tregaron and on further investigation by my hooded riders, we believe the Hugglett spoon, and maybe your parchments were in the chest. I AM SO SORRY. I do believe this is rightfully yours as Owain Glyndwr, seems to think. You'll find it and no harm will come to you. I hope by informing you of this incident, you can move forward in retrieving what is rightfully yours. Again, sorry for the mix-up.

TWM

"*Who is Twm Ivor?*" asked Molly thinking this was unbelievable information.

"**Twm Sion Cati** *as he's called is the local highwayman. He robs the rich and gives it to the poor. He happens to be Ivor's cousin,*" said Garibaldi losing patience.

"*Come on Molly we need to move the coracle before you go to Talley.*"

Molly left the cave with Slobbers and Yo-Yo by her side, the wizards sitting in their chairs looking decidedly sheepish. Tudor hadn't lied after all. The lanterns, chandeliers and all cave activity had resumed normality once the letter had been read. Bedivere knowing it was best to say nothing as did Elijas continued to put the paper puzzle together.

On the sand, Garibaldi had secured yellow buckets tied to poles, mimicking the coracle which was a few feet away.

"*You need to raise the coracle from the sand, turn it left and right and then it will move in the air towards the passage for us to hide it. You've already secured it, but to move it, you need to unleash it and give it your own spell. This will help us find it if it does disappear. With the news we have just received Molly I don't think this coracle should be on view after today,"* said Gari equally annoyed with Twm and Owain.

Molly nodded in agreement as Yo-Yo and Slobbers went further down the beach for a chat as they had a plan of their own that they needed to discuss.

"I'll demonstrate first," said Garibaldi.

The yellow bucket in front of Garibaldi looked as if it was standing to attention as Gari stood to the right of it, stretched his arm and hand out and muttered,

"Bwcedmelyn aros/ boo-ked-meh-leen –ah-ros," as he repeated three times.

The bucket untied itself from the stick and hovered ten inches above the sand.

"Ah-ros left" instructed Garibaldi,

The bucket turned left and right following Garibaldi's instructions.

"Ben-eeallee, lower, stop," the bucket stopped and hovered back to the ground.

"Easy Molly, now you do the same."

Molly stood in front of the same bucket,

"Bwcedmelyn aros/boo-ked-meh-leen," copied Molly.

Nothing.

"Ben-eealle, ben-eealle," she repeated.

Again nothing.

"I'm going to use my own spell Gari. Otherwise, we'll be here all night," said Molly getting frustrated. Surely, she was magical enough to administer a few spells. They were only buckets!

"Good idea," said Garibaldi sensing her frustration and total embarrassment.

"Ben-eeallee,   greegoloh," commanded Molly swishing her tail. The bucket unhinged from its stick, shook its head, and careered down the beach, without further ado. The same happened for the following few buckets and Garibaldi started to worry. Surely, Molly did have magical capabilities.

"There's only two buckets left Molly, try again."

"Bevan-eeallee, bevanali"

The two buckets together, rose from the sand,

"Will-ee-annie, greeg-oloh/ Williannie, Grigolo," she continued.

"La feh aros."

The buckets moved to the left and then right, hovering to the sand quietly and obediently.

"I think we need to trust your spells, Molly."

"I suggest we spell the coracle in readiness for Ivor to move her later," said Garibaldi satisfied Molly knew what she was doing if she used her own spells.

"Spell her to move on Ivor's command Molly. We need to get you away to see your folks and then we can place the coracle in the spare secret passage."

"*Suh-mend klu-wed Ivor,*" Molly repeated three times, as she swished her bushy tail, her glass eyes concentrating on the coracle, boring into its very ash seat as she repeated the spell again, sprinkling her dust from her tail as she chanted.

The coracle twitched as if acknowledging the command and Garibaldi satisfied, they could move the coracle right away, walked back to the cave with Molly.

"*Slobbers and Yo-Yo aren't on the beach Molly. I think they've gone to plan some support for you. We need to get you over to see your grandparents right away. The full moon's tomorrow, and if there's a message at the lake, that's when you're most likely to receive it,*" said Gari as he opened the cave door, to Bedivere and Elijas pouring over the puzzle in the corner.

"*Where's Ivor?*" asked Gari as he never left the cave without informing him.

"*He's seen movement on the hovel, those purple shadows, which we think are the new owners of the treasure chest, have stopped outside Tregaron again.*"

Garibaldi went to the parlour to investigate as Molly looked at the half-completed puzzle. The whole treasure hunt was about to get even more complicated; she just knew it. She wished they'd move the coracle, there was no urgency about the place at all.

***

Somewhere in Tregaron, a little boy had managed to open the treasure chest, which the kind man had given them. He'd been called away by his mother and had left the lid open. Something was wriggling at the bottom, trying to make a signal. The spoon was inside a silk pouch and was desperately trying to message the coracle.

Chapter 6

Cymberline.

Molly and Garibaldi arrived at the cave satisfied Ivor would move the coracle before nightfall. Molly decided to leave after lunch to Talley and she was in a dilemma on who to take with her. The security around the cave needed to be improved therefore it was prudent for her to go on her own. She felt that the wizards needed both Slobbers and Yo-Yo keeping watch.

"Do we have the hovel tracking for those Begglys, Gari?" asked Molly accepting a mug of tea from Ivor.

"No, but I can change that right away. I'll go and place you all on there, in readiness for your trip," said Gari feeling foolish, as that was an obvious thing to have done before now.

"The coach has left the tunnel, we need to move the coracle right away Ivor," said Geraintus as Molly nodded in agreement. There was a lack of urgency with Ivor, which was slightly disturbing.

"Yes, yes, let's see Molly on her way and we can move the coracle, finish that paper puzzle that Bedivere and Elijas have been working on. We should be a little closer to knowing at least where to go and search for this spoon," said Ivor sounding exasperated.

"Where are the Wizards?" asked Geraintus.

As Molly looked for Slobbers and Yo-Yo, the door opened, and they both came panting in.

"I suggested the Wizards went to fetch some overnight things," said Molly.

"Why so," said Ivor confused, which wasn't difficult.

"I think Bedivere and Elijas should stay here with Garibaldi, to oversee the coracle and wait for our return. I'll take Slobbers and Yo-Yo with me just in case I'm a target with the enemy."

The lantern turned white as the front door opened and both wizards returned with an overnight sac on each shoulder.

"I think it's too dangerous to go the regular route," said Ivor as Garibaldi returned from re-setting the hovel, with three, **"double pins"** in his hand.

"I agree," said Bedivere sitting next to the incomplete puzzle. *"We could take you to Caldey Island at dawn. The monks will put you on the scuttle ship to Llanelli. It's a long way round, but I think it's too dangerous now for you to risk travelling the usual way. From Llanelli, you can meet the Stradey Arms coach, like our Three Feathers which will take you to Llandeilo. You'll have to find your own way from there, but it's only six miles or so. If we pebble them tonight, they'll be able to meet you in Llandeilo, I'm sure."*

Coracle on the beach with Slobbers the cat

"*I'm not letting you go alone,*" said Gari holding out the double pins. "*I've coded these pins to the hovel, which means I'll be able to keep track of you.*"

"*Yes, Slobbers and Yo-Yo are both coming that's why I wanted Bedivere and Elijas to stay here tonight,*" assured Molly. "*I know Geraintus is keeping an eye out on the beach, which leaves you Gari to watch the hovel for any odd movements.*"

Slobbers and Yo-Yo's relief was evident as they'd both had already decided they were going with her.

"*I know Wibbly Alf from the Edwinsford Arms, I'll send my own pebble to warn him,*" said Slobbers feeling excited once again.

"*I'm not happy,*" said Ivor, "*We need a magical creature protecting us.*"

"*Why don't we ask Tudor if he can send Kester, his bat down for a day or two? He seems ingenious,*" suggested Molly.

"*No, we can't,*" said Ivor looking a bit confused and needed to give some information that he knew to the family. He wasn't as weak as they all made out; he was more magical at times. Even surprising himself.

"*Why not?*" asked Molly sounding impatient with Ivor as he seemed permanently pre-occupied with something.

"*Tudor is receiving visitors in a few hours. Bethesda the minister from St. Clears is arriving to discuss the arrangements for the singing festival, which he's never done before. Something isn't quite right there,"* said Ivor. *"Firstly, Bethesda never stays the night, and the song contest doesn't involve us. He is also taking his dog Millie with him which again he never normally takes the dog anywhere."*

"What difference does it make him taking Millie?" asked Molly.

"She's a magical dog, there's a bit of history there but we need Kester to keep an eye on the castle whilst Bethesda is visiting."

"Bethesda's one of the people at Kentav Croggs' hutlet who was at the meeting after the town hall," confirmed Slobbers.

"I think Kester, should stay there if that's the case. We need to keep an eye on Tudor, even though he's not a spy. Slobbers and Yo-Yo can stay here, and I will go to Talley by myself. No one will expect that, and this will make me less conspicuous."

*"**NO**,"* shouted both Yo-Yo and Slobbers together as Molly smiled and realised, she was obviously key to this family and needed to get results quickly.

"Garibaldi, you need to lock yourselves in for the night and we will leave right away. Geraintus patrol outside and change the status of the cave to outline. Ivor, please move the coracle right away to the tunnel and let's hope you don't get attacked whilst we're away. With the cave in outline mode, it should make it temporarily invisible," suggested Molly eager to get moving.

"Let me place these *"**Double pins**"* on your coats and then ...."

HISS...HISS...HISS

"*It's the hovel quick, what's happening.*"

"*Molly get ready I shall find out,*" said Garibaldi getting a bit worried about unexplained activities at that moment.

CRASH, CRASH, CRASH

The lantern in the hallway crashed to the floor as everyone jumped in shock. The purple curling smoke bellowed out of the cracked top as the chandeliers above turned purple and started jangling as if trying to warn someone about something.

Elijas, who was getting very frustrated by the lack of urgency with this magical bunch, went to gather up the broken glass, yet again, using his own spell. He wasn't sure that any of these wizards had any substance. He'd wait and see what would transpire after Molly's visit to Talley.

"*Goodness me,*" remarked Ivor getting in a muddle with his colour codes as he scanned behind the door for the significance of the purple colour. "*There's something going on, this hasn't happened before.*"

"*It's the hovel, those purple shadows are moving, and we think they've got the treasure chest. The sooner you leave Molly the better. You ought to fly towards the area where these travellers are, they have the chest. At least we will have the two main treasures then. We'll only need to find the right parchments and we will be done.*"

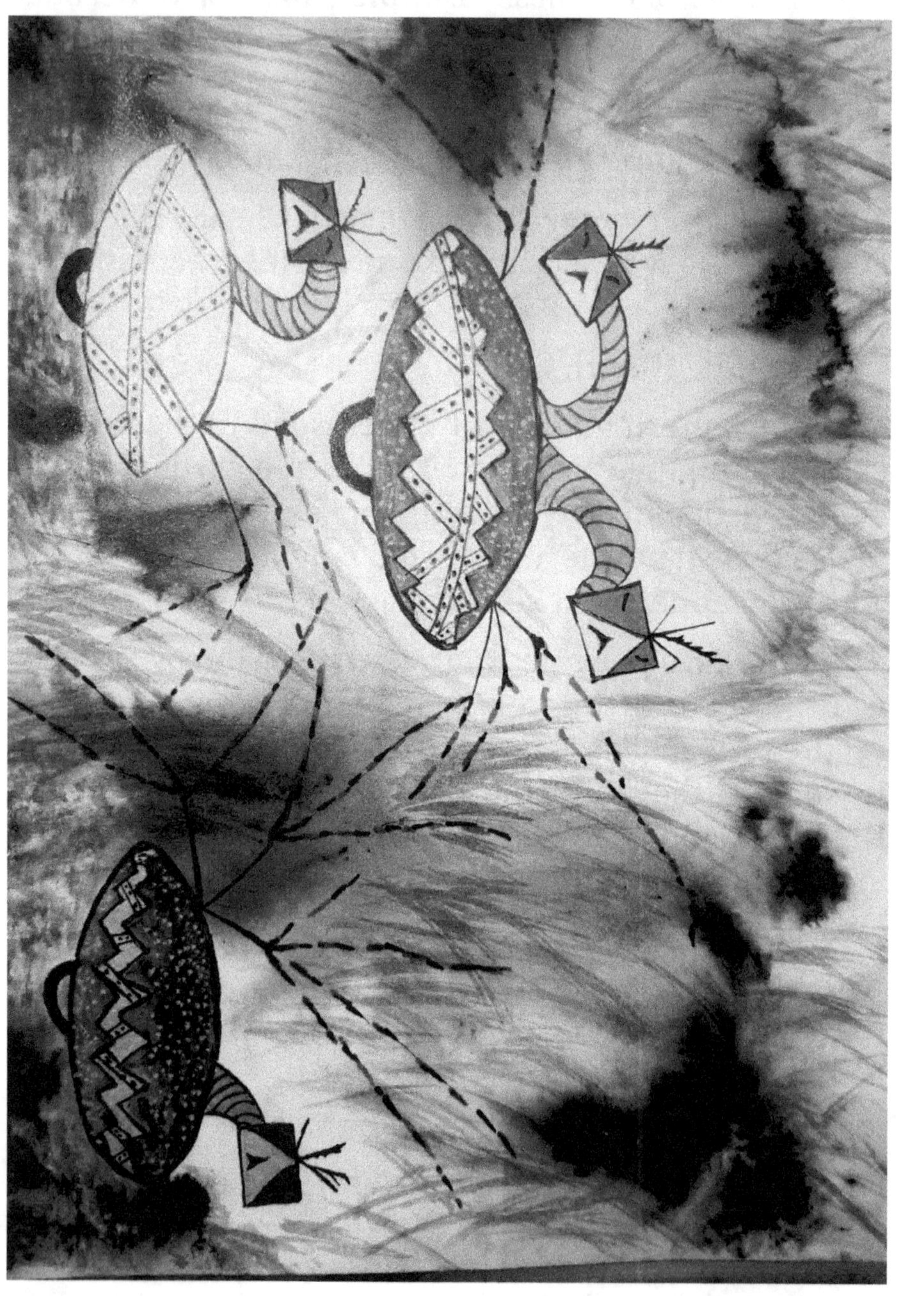

Beggly army

"I think Molly needs to visit Talley right away and before she makes that decision, she needs to contact us," suggested Bedivere. *"We will have completed the puzzle by then and we may have more information at hand for her."*

"In the meantime," Ivor suggested, *"The second passage is ready for you to leave right away. The monks at Caldey Island are waiting. We shall get on with things here and move the coracle."*

"Yes, Ivor the coracle needs to be away from the beach as soon as we leave," said Molly as she flung her cape on her shoulders, helped by Yo-Yo. Slobbers had a few things for them in an overnight sac which included some communication pebbles.

"Take us to the tunnel," said Molly ready to get on with some action.

The secret passage was open, and it looked like a whitewashed round house with no windows. They went inside as Bedivere, and Ivor gave Molly their instructions. The tunnel gate was closed, and Molly grabbed Slobbers' tail as he did Yo-Yo, and they were as one. Molly murmured the spell,

"Jem-Bali bail-eeonee/Gembali beillioni," she repeated several times as the tunnel turned upside down and careered itself downwards turning them clockwise rapidly making them all catch their breath. Before Yo-Yo could think of shaking some more, the tunnel stopped, and they landed outside the cave entrance of the Chief Monk Caldey.

Chief Monk Caldey didn't look happy as three animals bundled out of the tunnel at the foot of the caves of Caldey Island.

"Come with me, the scuttle ship's about to leave, we must hurry."

Around the corner moored a magnificent ship, its sails up, all ready to depart. The ship was delivering the Monk's supply of honey and perfume which was made on the island under a secret contract with Owain Glyndwr.

"Here is the schedule of the next four ships which will be at Llanelli docks over the next four weeks, should you need to use this means of transport," said the Monk handing Molly a parchment which Slobbers took from her for safe keeping.

"Thank you," said Molly.

"Is Bedivere or Ivor with you at any stage?" he asked.

"Not to our immediate knowledge," said Molly learning that being vague was her best option.

They followed the Monk on to the ship and were given the top deck. The three of them jumped onto the two hammocks as Yo-Yo snuggled under Molly's belly. They relaxed and this gave Molly time to think about the general state of the family.

"Why is Bethesda at Tudor's in Caernarvon Slobbers? What's going on there?"

"Funny you should bring that up Molly, but I was just thinking the same."

"Is there anything I need to know Slobbers, which right now may be the best time to tell me the secrets these wizards seem to have. You do realise this could affect their magic, and it's nothing to do with retrieving the spoon and chest. If they're not true to their past, it may be affecting their futuristic spell powers."

CLANG CLANG CLANG

The dinner gong sounded before Slobbers could answer Molly's question. A servant came into view and laid down food for them, along with water bowls.

"Slobbers," said Molly suddenly her instincts kicking in.

"Send a pebble to Gari immediately."

Slobbers untied the sack from under his belly as Molly laughed, the gentle snores from the hammock as Yo-Yo was still asleep, not being affected by Molly and Slobbers chatting.

"I thought you were just a big cat Slobbers. I didn't realise you had a pouch full of goodies under your tummy."

"I quite like for them all to think that, Molly. The less we tell them the better, until we can marry this treasure together. They're losing their abilities, what do you want to instruct Garibaldi?" as Slobbers took out an orange pebble for Molly to dictate her message.

"Watch Kester and Millie the dog at Caernarvon Castle."

"Will Gari understand what I'm trying to say?" asked Molly anxious her first pebble was going to make sense.

"Yes, Gari is ahead of us all. He'll understand, shall send it now."

A wave of Slobbers' tail and a seagull flew onto the edge of the ship.

"Gerald for Garibaldi, as quick as you can," instructed Slobbers as he attached the pebble onto the gulls' ruffled feathers.

"Will send Gertrude to cover whilst I'm gone," he squawked and disappeared before Molly could say thank you.

"Before we get to Talley Slobbers," said Molly as they watched Yo-Yo wake up and jump out of the hammock to eat his dinner. *"What's this about Millie the retriever and her history. What did Gari mean?"*

"Millie was found by Bethesda or one of the Croggs, whilst the family were in one of their numerous past battles. Anyway, the Croggs claimed her as theirs and she was given to Bethesda to look after. She has magical qualities, and I believe she's ours but the wizards at the time didn't have any proof that she's a Llewellyn dog."

"Does she know?"

"Yes, I believe so ,but currently she's no powers to swap sides, which would be licensed to get banished as

they did to their fourth brother. She needs to have good reason to defect. We just need to keep an eye on her that's all."

"I see," said Molly realising there was a lot of unfinished or unattended business within the business of this lost treasure.

"Who is Wibbly Alf?" asked Yo-Yo joining the two on the hammock wanting to know if there was another dog or cat to think about.

"He's a great big St. Bernard," said Slobbers waving his long tail in the air and smiling at Yo-Yo. *"He's a calm dog, he's very astute, and he'll be able to help us. Last year, he was instrumental in finding Garibaldi's green hats that had gone missing. They'd been stolen and were in Pumpsaint, near the gold mines. Wibbly and his street friends went on a mission and found them, and we've been friends ever since. We need these friends everywhere as they keep us informed via our kites. This helps us get ahead of the average family when there is a problem."*

"That's good we have contacts everywhere. We need them too," Molly sighed as she had her own unfinished business and hoped it wasn't too long before she could share her own demons with Slobbers and Ivor. Hopefully, these extra magical animals could eventually help her personally too.

***

Back at the cave, the paper puzzle was complete, and the two wizards were pouring over the information. Garibaldi was tracking the hovel and was disturbed as there wasn't sign of that magical dog Millie, who was meant to accompany Bethesda. Tudor had received him but no dog.

***

The scuttle ship arrived at Llanelli and the three of them descended having changed their collars for day ones. To date Molly had stuck to the purple one, even though she'd been asked by Ivor to wear the red collar.

Yo-Yo whispered the spell as the Stradey coach screeched to a halt having hovered over the docks waiting.

"Velez Rubio," he commanded as the glass doors opened and the steps shot out of the coach. The three feathers like Ivor's coach twitched at the top of the crater sensing the urgency. Slobbers and Molly jumped on to the plush interior cushions as the coach lifted quickly and started its journey towards Llandeilo. The landing spot was the Cawdor Arms hotel, as there was a wedding going on at the church.

***

A convoy of animals in a horse drawn carriage were already waiting outside the hotel for Magical Molly and her friends' arrival.

Crogg Hutlets

Chapter 7

The Beggly creature.

"**Q**UIET, *all of you,*" shouted Harry the horse. *"You must be a bit more orderly than this; whatever will Molly think of us?"*

He stomped his legs in agitation and everyone on board the cart fell silent. They were just excited to convoy Molly back to her grandparents.

The cart was 'chock a block' full of animals and how they were going to fit an extra three, Harry had no idea. Harry only wished that Willie and Annie had been a bit more organised, but then they'd only received the urgent pebble that morning. Therefore, all of this had been arranged in haste.

Harry looked over his shoulder as they waited. The only sensible breeds of animal in the cart were dogs. It was always dogs as far as he was concerned but then the cat contingent had never failed to amaze him either. In the cart were the three border collies that worked for Willie and Annie and the two black Labradors that lived next door. They had insisted on coming along with their children for the adventure. One of the puppies was intensely chewing the side of the cart ignoring the others who were scampering over everyone, playing. They'd been joined by the four white geese, who acted as pebble deliverers in the area and three floppy-eared rabbits that pretended to be pet rabbits in the pub. The two ginger cats who were twins, sat on Harry's mane looking out for everyone and above them, clucking furiously warning them that the coach was imminent was Gertrude, the white hen.

Gertrude always clucked if something was amiss and for years now, the ginger twins had delivered an egg a day to her nest. The farmer would kill her for his table if he knew she was a magical hen and not a domestic one.

The dog's presence was to ensure nothing happened to Gertrude, as they all remembered the last disaster when it had taken all five dogs to pin her down, from her last assignment.

***

The Stradey arms coach was approaching as Molly instructed Yo-Yo to brush her coat with angel dust and to loosen her purple collar. For some reason, it had started to tingle again. Slobbers and Yo-Yo were also sprinkled with dust, and they were ready.

The oval glass coach came to an abrupt halt in the car park of the hotel and Slobbers clocked the cats sitting on the horse as he questioned,

"Molly, I presume that horse along with the cats are waiting for us. There are a few collies in the cart too."

"Yes, let's go," said Molly anxious to get under way before anyone noticed a weird looking glass coach.

The steps threw themselves towards the ground as Yo-Yo, curled in a ball plopped down ahead of them as Slobbers allowed Molly to go first. Before the coach had time to disappear there was a big cheer from everyone as they ran towards them, all stopping at the fur ball in front of Molly.

"Welcome all of you, let's go," said one of the border collies as Yo-Yo unravelled joining them in step.

"I'll join the cats on Harry," suggested Slobbers as he wanted to gather intelligence immediately of the area.

All the animals shuffled up as Molly and Yo-Yo jumped in the back and they were quickly covered with fur of some kind or another, the camouflage working perfectly.

The journey to the Edwinsford Arms was not a long one although the windy roads and sharp bends made the trip a bit bumpy. At one point, one of the floppy-eared rabbits fell out from a bump and one of the Labradors jumped out and picked it up by its furry neck and put it back on the cart.

Molly's excitement grew as they got nearer; she hadn't seen her grandparents for over two years. They were waiting at the pub, with their own cart to take them down the rugged lane towards the lakes, where their owners had a cottage and a farm.

Harry trotted into the pub car park and immediately one of the cats tied him up loosely at his designated pole. Slobbers and the Ginger twins were already pals and had made some plan as Molly's excitement showed as she became overwhelmed by the moment.

Willie and Annie came bounding out from the barn followed by Wibbly Alf as Molly embraced them. Slobbers and Yo-Yo were close behind her, with Yo-Yo carrying her overnight sack.

Wibbly Alf introduced himself to Molly and the others and they all departed quickly as advised by Slobbers, who already had something on his mind. Wibbly Alf was designated to pull the cart, and they all jumped on. Gertrude the hen continued to cluck overhead.

Wibbly Alf, a St. Bernard, was chocolate brown in colour. He had a white chest and an unusual chain around his neck which was noticeable, but as Yo-Yo made comment; Wibbly said he would explain later.

Slobbers was uneasy and on alert as the ginger cats had made a comment that there was something wrong. Gertrude had continued to cluck from the moment they'd arrived in Llandeilo. This was unusual and Slobbers went ahead as Molly sat on the cart with her family. Yo-Yo picked up there was something amiss and started to run back and forth too. Molly aware something wasn't right continued to stay calm, but she knew too that something was wrong.

***

Back at the cave, the paper puzzle was a source of considerable debate as the wizards were trying to make some sense of the clues.

Garibaldi was anxious as he tried to send an urgent pebble to Slobbers as he'd discovered through the hovel, a presence in the barn of the Talley lakes. This was not a family member. To add insult to injury the chandeliers in the cave alongside the lantern were turning black in colour, a dangerous signal for the wizards and one they couldn't control. He felt quite helpless as something wasn't right. He was also struggling with finding the retriever who was meant to be with Bethesda at Caernarvon Castle, as yet she hadn't been spotted anywhere.

His most frightening problem right now was Ivor. He had forgotten the spell Molly had instructed and given him, to remove the coracle from the beach. Even Bedivere couldn't help him remember. Geraintus was out patrolling, but Garibaldi had that feeling of dread in the pit of his stomach, only he knew what that meant.

***

Willie and Annie welcomed Molly and her entourage to their humble barn as the family caught up with all their news. Willie and Annie were careful not to mention Molly's own demons, as they weren't sure if she'd told anyone.

"The lady at the lake may come out tonight, as it's a full moon," said Willie. *"We're convinced that she'll have something to tell you."*

"How do you know this?" asked a curious Yo-Yo as a pebble plopped at Slobbers' feet for him to read.

Willie continued to explain as Slobbers quietly read his pebble.

"Cymberline is her name, and she'd married a "princely" farmer. Her father had warned him that if he ever struck her three times with an iron, she would walk into the lake and drown herself. The marriage was a happy one, but the farmer did strike her three times and on the third occasion, she walked into the lake and drowned. The farmer was beside himself and tried to stop her, followed her with his tractor and plough attached to his subsequent death. There are still tractor marks at the edge of the lake to this day.

Cymberline hasn't rested in peace to this day. She sometimes rises from the depths of the lake under full moon, with prophecies and future tales of happenings as if she's warning people of their fate.

When your parents left, Cymberline told them that their first born, which is you Molly will be gifted and save the family of all evil. I think we should all accompany you, unless you think you should see if she appears, by yourself."

"No, there's a problem, Molly needs to stay here, until I return," said Slobbers butting in having read the pebble. *"Yo-Yo, stay with Molly until I get back."*

"What is it?" asked Molly knowing something wasn't right, as her collar had continued tingling.

"It's that bug dog, we've a spy. I need to go and deal with it; at no cost should you get involved as they believe you're important enough to be followed."

Slobbers sent the pebble back to Gari, confirming they had a spy in the vicinity and would deal with it. Slobbers made his way back to the pub very quickly to discuss the problem. He didn't think to check the barn next door to Molly's family as the bug dog spied on him, recognised him as the cat that had attacked him and decided to follow him.

Slobbers was uneasy, he didn't want another encounter with the bug dog and the sooner he got to the pub the better. The Ginger Cats were waiting for him, along with Wibbly Alf and they went inside the barn quickly. Harry stuck his head out of the top door and Ginger Two sat on his mane to keep watch.

"Do we have a sighting yet?" asked Ginger One taking charge of the proceedings.

"CLUCK, CLUCK, CLUCK."

"Doesn't she ever stop making such a din?" asked Slobbers trying to think of a plan.

"That's just it Slobbers, the creature is close by which is why she's clucking like mad. We need to know about him, in order we can eliminate him. We know you fought him at St Clears, we need to get rid of him before nightfall."

"He's like a machine; he's three antennae on the top of his oval body. He's quite heavy, can't get up like us but equally he's fast. When he spins, he sends out sparks like lightning which sting. He can fire the sparks so much; it will kill whoever is on the receiving end. He didn't expect me to jump on him; I bent one of his antennae

which meant I was able to walk away. He's quite scary and the Croggs have hundreds of them, they're breeding like rabbits."

"*What else do you know?*" asked Wibbly feeling a bit uncomfortable with this knowledge.

"*They've been well trained; it seems once they're given instruction they'll not stop until that task is done.*"

"*How are they in the water Slobbers?*" asked Ginger Two from Harry's mane.

"*No idea why, what are you thinking?*"

"*Slobbers, if they're more mechanical than animal, surely all we need to do is drown it?*"

"*How do you propose we do that?*" asked Slobbers not really wanting to fight with this creature again.

"*If we can drown him that's better than him finding out anything at the lake. Even if we find him, he could hide and then he might program all the information he can hear from the lake. This is assuming Cymberline will appear tonight. However, he'll take the information back to the Croggs and they might decipher any riddle quicker than us. Please bear in mind the wizards are losing their abilities as we speak.*"

"*How do we propose we kill him?*"

"*Gertrude is clucking so much I can only imagine the creature isn't too far from us. Why don't you pretend all is well Slobbers, make your way back to the lake and Ginger and I will follow. Wibbly Alf here will run round the long way but will get to the first barn before you. If you go inside, leave the barn door open as that creature will follow you in wanting to finish you off this time."*

Slobbers tried not to squirm at this comment but Ginger One was right.

"Wibbly Alf will have gone ahead and set up a trap in the barn, all you need to do is make sure you're being followed. Once he's in the barn, let us deal with him, you've already suffered but survived from his attack and we know you are an exceptional fighter at the best of times."

Slobbers grew twice the size having been told he was this brave cat, he certainly didn't feel very brave at all, but he wasn't going to let the team down. He was Molly's Top Cat, and he needed to step up and prove it.

Wibbly got up to go and sort the smaller cart as Slobbers yet again noticed his chain as it was twinkling quietly underneath his thick chocolate brown chest. He couldn't help but ask the question there and then as he was drawn to it for some reason.

"Wibbly what's with this link chain? You said that this was quite important, and I keep hearing it twinkle am I going mad?"

"No, you're not going mad at all," said Wibbly. *"I found it near Tregaron racetracks; we were doing some reconnaissance work when we found out that Molly was coming over. Look at the chain Slobbers, it's quite detailed; we think it has something to do with the family but we're not sure."*

Silk pouch

Slobbers was in awe as he looked at the intricate detail of the chain. The hooks attached to the links appeared to be worn and had obviously been linked to something before getting lost. The links themselves had intricate carvings amongst them, there was a bird and a coracle and an outline of a dog.

"What does this mean?" he asked as Wibbly motioned they needed to get going.

"We've no idea Slobbers but since Wibbly has worn it, Gertrude hasn't stopped clucking."

"I think Wibbly needs to be at the lake, something tells me this is part of the Llewellyn treasure. Don't ask me why but I have spent so much time with the wizards and Garibaldi to sense this link chain is critical," said Slobbers getting excited and feeling a bit faint at the same time. *"Ginger One, can you discreetly fetch Yo-Yo as I think we ought to take Harry and the big cart with us. If we've part of the missing spoons link chain, it's best we all stick together and fight this Beggly, protect Molly and get back to Ivor's cave quickly. We'll tell Molly later but for now Wibbly keeps this chain round his neck. It's far safer there than anywhere else and then we can look at it properly when we get back to Ivor's."*

Within minutes of this discovery and giving Ginger One instruction, Ginger Two appeared through the trapdoor with a ball of fur in his mouth as he dropped Yo-Yo to the ground. He unravelled and found himself staring into Wibbly's thick chocolate mane and swallowed the lump in this throat a bit daunted.

"Ok," said Slobbers as he realised, he was with a team of magical creatures even more efficient than his wizards back at the cave. He got quite excited about this prospect, and they huddled together planning. Gertrude flew round the barn clucking softly as Harry nodded his head, listening and watching at the same time. She'd got the point across that the bug dog was spying across the road and was waiting for their next move.

***

Back at Ivor's cave there was plenty going on. Pebbles were arriving at various speeds and the two wizards were at loggerheads. One wanted to go and assist the goings on in Talley and the other was worried that he'd forgotten all his spells. As their argument reached a crescendo, the miner's lantern, which was normally an orange colour depicting a tranquil state, turned into curling black smoke. The smoke curled into the dining room, sending everyone coughing and spluttering outside.

It was too late; the smoke was telling them that there was trouble. They couldn't go and help Molly as their biggest problem, was simply theirs. They couldn't remember the spell Molly had given them. To add insult to injury Garibaldi had found the enemy on his hovel and knew it was too late to send help. They would have to sort out the problem; he had enough on his plate here.

***

Slobbers sauntered quickly but less confident than he looked towards the lake. The plan was in place, and he moved deftly as it was quite dark now. This had to work as soon the full moon would be at its height and they would be late for the lakeside ritual. Yo-Yo went with Harry and the cart as he needed to warn Molly. Wibbly had hidden in the cart along with the cats as they needed to be in the second barn in advance of Slobbers. Gertrude was quiet for a change and was flying overhead of Slobbers like his guardian angel. This comforted Slobbers a bit as he knew he was being followed by the bug dog; Gertrude's silence was his signal.

As they'd guessed the bug dog followed Slobbers into the second barn and immediately the barn door and latch were put in place by the Ginger twins. Slobbers threw himself into the haystack and covered hay over him quickly as the two brown heifers nodded their heads. He made his way up towards and through the skylight, and he was on the tree branch within minutes. Harry and the cart which was now laden with coal prevented the barn door from opening. The sparks from the antennae of the bug dog started lashing the door but Harry stood his ground the cart sometimes jolting with the electric shock from the creature.

Slobbers held his breath; the moon was rising to position as he saw Molly and Yo-Yo walk towards the lake with Wibbly. He waited until he was satisfied the heifers had trampled on the bug dog enough to kill him. Once dead or as near to death, he and the Gingers would finish him in the lake, drowning him was the final plan. He hoped.

The noise from the barn depicted the heifers had done their job as the Gingers whistled for Slobbers. Slobbers slid down the tree quickly and joined them, they opened the barn door, and the heifer threw out the creature looking mangled, his antennae broken and his body in pieces.

"Quick. Throw him on the cart," said Slobbers as Harry had transformed the cart again to empty.

"We need to drown him right away as the lake is swelling, before the lady of the lake appears," said Slobbers, quite relieved to see a bug dog in bits. They all jumped into the cart and Harry trotted down to the lakeside away from Molly's party for a moment to finish the job.

Chapter 8

The lady of the lake.

Molly was reassured at the depth of magical attributes the animals had around her and was secretly grateful as it helped her confidence. She knew that if this lady came out of the lake, she would help them find the missing spoon. Molly wore her night collar which Yo-Yo had swopped for her earlier. He was standing by her side by the lake as she realised as she looked over her shoulder that the Ginger twins along with Slobbers had arrived with Harry.

Molly guessed what had happened, she was pleased by her own psychic abilities, but that's why the family had asked for her. She had to remember that she was the most magical dog to be born to the Llewellyn family; this surely had to be an asset for when her own family needed to be saved. Yo-Yo interrupted her thoughts.

"Molly, look the lake is swelling and ooohh........"

The full moon shone as bright as the sun as it moved closer overhead to the edge of the lake. The brightness highlighted the row of animals sitting by the lake. Molly's grandparents and the neighbour's dogs, sitting behind, protecting them. The three border collies would be decoys if Molly needed to disappear back into the barn. They were ready. Suddenly as the moon glowered over the lake, a black swirling cloud appeared from the water and a mist descended over everyone.

From the middle of the lake rose a figure dressed in a white chiffon gown and she drifted towards the party waiting at the edge. Yo-Yo tried to swallow a lump in his throat and went to hide beneath Molly as the woman floated closer. Molly walked forward and stood in the water, her tail was erect and glowed orange as if inviting her over. Yo-Yo moved closer to Slobbers.

The lady was smiling with her arms outstretched and welcomed the party at the edge of the lake. She stared right into Molly's eyes and whispered distinctly to her, not pausing for breath before she disappeared as quickly as she'd appeared. No one moved as she talked.

"Death is imminent for a friend and not a foe; use your magical, mystical power and mystical spell. Eagles are coming; red kites or bats; no. Find the clue, an ancient place with a wishing well. Purple is strong, but there's turquoise blue. Not to paddle but carry Coracle Gold. Nesta, Helen of Wales, says it's true. Treasure chest needs to be found and sold, Magical, Mystical Molly, it's written in the mud. You or your friends mustn't shed the first blood!"

The swirling black cloud disappeared once Cymberline had gone, and the lake returned to normal. No one moved as Slobbers cringed thinking they'd already killed a creature and did that count?

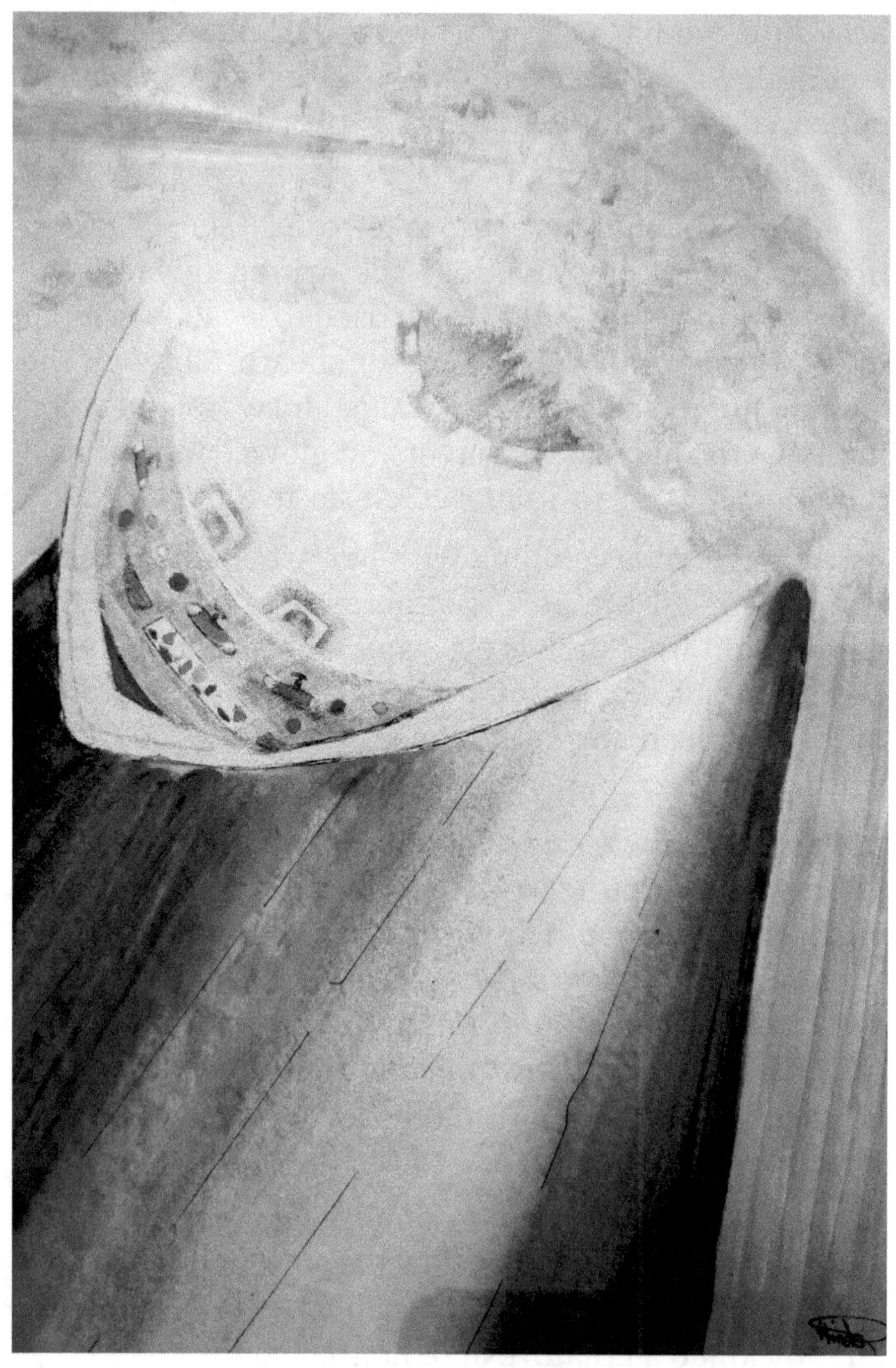

Moonbeam arriving

Molly's collar started to tingle, and she knew that this was another sign. They all followed her as she made her way back to the barn. They needed to talk about this riddle. There were a few clues in the poem and a plan on their next move was imminent.

Slobbers sent a pebble right away to Garibaldi, he needed to inform the wizards of the riddle, and he hoped that they'd have a suggestion on their next move.

"I'm not sure we need to visit this Twm Sion Cati fellow right now. We know he has interfered with our treasure hunt; he can't add any value to our mission. What do you all think?" asked Molly wanting some help on what to do next.

"We need to work fast," said Wibbly as everyone agreed even Harry, who had his head stuck through the top door.

"You need to call the coach, Slobbers, we need to leave. We need to get back to the cave, discuss this with the wizards, and decide from there," said Molly.

"Wibbly needs to come with you as this link chain Molly needs to be attached to the golden coracle," said Willie as he showed them all why there were hooks on the chain.

"This is the link chain that no one's aware is missing," said Willie who was truly knowledgeable within family matters. *"We recognised it as soon as Wibbly showed us. The thing is Wibbly Alf is carrying it without affecting its powers as it's as clever as the Hugglett spoon. Molly, I think Wibbly should go with you as extra protection. He*

is a Llewellyn and the chain round his neck is a good as disguise as any to keep it away from the enemy,"

"I'm coming too," said Ginger One and Two together as Molly smiled.

"Will the wizards have more powers passed to them if we can take a spoon to them right away?" asked Molly as Slobbers looked at her. They both knew that this was a critical question.

"No not really, the wizards need the coracle and spoon linked to each other by this chain to give them the powers they're losing. The quicker you decipher the riddle with the wizards the quicker you can help them," said Annie.

Harry brayed from the door as the coach was arriving in minutes to take them to their next destination.

"Let's wait, to see what Gari thinks," suggested Slobbers. *"I've sent him a pebble; it's worth hanging on to see what he suggests as we seem to be all going with Molly."*

***

Back at the cave, the wizards were pleased as they'd finished the puzzle. However, Ivor was exasperated as he was still trying to remember the spell, to move the coracle from the beach. Bedivere had also eaten the entire seventh batch of Welsh cakes and he was hungry.

"Gari, can you make more Welsh cakes. Look we've finished the puzzle; it's a map of Carmarthenshire and district with all the castles marked."

"I'll have a look in a minute," said Gari as he whisked away into the kitchen. He appeared by magic with a plate of Welsh cakes piled high and a respective plate of chocolate biscuits to keep them going. It was challenging work keeping them awake and occupied knowing that they were too old for this excitement until they received an influx of power from the missing treasure.

"It's a map of the castles, what are the missing torn bits you've got left?" asked Gari intrigued by this. He'd been pre-occupied with keeping an eye on Tudor in Caernarvon Castle, as there was still no sign of the missing retriever that Kester was searching for. He'd also been worried about the enemy he'd seen on the hovel at the lakes. Before he could make a comment there was a knock on the door.

RAT-TAT-TAT

The miners' lamp had gone white as Gari accepted the pebble from the goose.

"From Slobbers."

Ivor looked uneasy as Bedivere stopped eating biscuits as they watched Gari read the message and re-read it again. He fetched a quill from Ivor's bureau and wrote down the riddle.

"What is it Gari?"

Glass coach & YoYo

"Cymberline came out of the lake and gave them a riddle. I'll read it to you in a minute. I must send a pebble of instructions to Molly first and then we can decide what to do."

Gari swiftly sent a pebble to Slobbers and then read out the riddle for the wizards.

*"Goodness Gracious me, they must go straight to see Robin and Rudge at **Bwlch Nant yr Arian** near Tregaron, said Ivor."*

"Yes, I've suggested this already, the pebble's gone," said Gari thankful he was ahead of them.

"Why don't we finish off these torn bits of paper and then we can see if they relate to this riddle," said Bedivere anxious to get a plan underway. He was even more concerned with Ivor as the coracle was still outside and they knew it was at risk. He also knew that Gari was feeling quite helpless as normally Gari was able to jog Ivor's memory, but not at this moment. Bedivere only hoped if they finished the torn bits of paper, something might trigger Ivor's memory.

"Yes, do that and I will try and remember the spell for the coracle," said Ivor as he went to his quarters to look for his shepherd's stick. If he could find his stick it would help as the twisted candles around the stick normally jogged his memory. He knew he had to sort this out quickly as Molly wouldn't be overly impressed if he had to admit he'd forgotten. He knew that Garibaldi wasn't too pleased with him right now either, but he also knew that Gari was worried too.

"The sooner you read this riddle Bedivere, the quicker you may be able to help me sort Ivor out. That coracle must be inside, I'm worried. Look what the poem says about it," said Gari handing Bedivere the parchment.

"Oh dear," said Bedivere as he read, ***"Not to paddle, but carry, Coracle Gold."***

"What does that mean I wonder? Let me decipher this, call Ivor Gari, and send Molly instructions to visit the kites at once."

"Already done Bedivere. I'll fetch Ivor. In fact, this riddle might jog his memory."

Elijas who had been deep in thought and fiddling with the torn papers, looked up and announced, pleased with himself,

"Done, look they're all words and there's a couple of letters."

As Elijas announced his achievement Ivor strode into the dining room, his pleated cloak flapping. The triple cuffed sleeve rolled back over his shoulder as he held his shepherds' stick, pleased at last.

"Found it."

"Let's hope you can remember the spell then," said Garibaldi as he returned from the parlour checking the hovel as he announced that Molly and gang were leaving Talley.

***

Somewhere in Tudor's Caernarvon Castle, Kester the bat was still trying to locate the golden retriever that had mysteriously not appeared. Unknown to Ivor and his wizards, there was someone in one of their secret passages in the cave, who currently was too weak to make contact.

***

The Edwinsford pub car park was crowded as the animals all sat in the cart waiting for the Stradey coach to whirl towards them. It had been spotted earlier dropping off a knight at the Cawdor Inn, Llandeilo. Everyone was coming with Molly and there had been an intense argument with the Ginger twins and Harry. Molly eventually gave in, and they had all quietened down and were saying goodbye to Will and Annie. Gertrude clucked flying round them, insistent that she was also coming along.

"We'll keep in touch Molly," said Willie as he and Annie stood back as the coach flew into the yard, its spindly legs and claws eager to land. There was no time to waste as the glass steps threw themselves out of the side as everyone looked on, but no one moved.

Molly smiled as she could see why, the steps were narrow and the entrance to the coach was not very wide either. She could sense everyone was wondering how they were going to come along. Harry was insistent that even the cart was coming as Molly went forward.

PLOP-PLOP-PLOP

"Molly, a red pebble before you spell the coach," said Slobbers.

"What's the message?" asked Molly.

"Tregaron fair, Robin and Rudge must be informed about Cymberline, don't use scuttle ship, use coach."

"We're just about to do that," said Yo-Yo getting agitated as they were taking too much time.

"Molly, Gari is guiding us; let's go Harry's trap is now going to be perfect cover for Tregaron. I'll explain once we get in the coach," said Slobbers as Molly started to prepare the coach for them to alight.

"Wear the red collar, that Ivor gave us," said Yo-Yo.

"Ok," said Molly wanting to get on with it. She stood in front of the coach and her tail went straight up as she beckoned for the animals to come to her.

"Tails," she instructed as everyone grabbed each other's tails making a circle. Gertrude flew in the centre; her clucking had stopped.

"Vitagliano pelygrus Pelygroso/ Veet agh leeanoh pale-eegrosso."

She swished her tail three times, scattering angel dust from her tail over herself and everyone in the circle. She looked up and realised that everyone was red and upside down.

"Oh gosh no."

"Vitagliano pelygrus Pelygroso, maritims ryfeddol benilali- Veetak-leeano pail-uh-grees pehlee-gross-oh

mareetems ruh-vethole ben-eealee," as she repeated three times.

She looked up and to her amazement everyone had shrank to size and were all scampering up the steps without further ado. They used the trap as a sofa, and they sat around Molly and Slobbers for their new instructions.

Wibbly Alf had sussed out the controls very quickly with Yo-Yo and they had twenty minutes before they'd arrive in Tregaron. The coach three feathers radar system twitched and rose towards the hedges and skimmed the hedgerows as it purred towards their destination.

"Right, everyone; there's a pony and trap event in Tregaron right now and Harry and his cart will be perfect cover. We need to see Robin and Rudge who are red kites. Gertrude, you can fly to them in advance. I'm going to give you all jobs as we need to see how much information we can gather before we get back to Ivor. Harry, you need to trot round as if you were entering the competition."

The two Ginger cats were plaiting his mane as Molly was giving out instructions.

"I think Slobbers and the twins should go wandering round the town to see if there's a sign of a treasure chest anywhere."

"Yo-Yo, Wibbly, we'll go to see the kites and gather information from them. I'll spell us before we leave the coach; we will all have two hours to get back to Harry's

cart. Harry, you'll make your way to Saundersfoot by road if something happens and we don't get back in time. At no cost you wait for me or anyone. The sooner we get there and leave the sooner we can help the wizards regain their memory. Everyone ok with this?"

They all nodded as Slobbers came back from the dashboard.

"We're about to land, everyone get ready."

The coach slowed down and hovered three feet from the ground as the steps flung themselves in the air suspended as everyone jumped out. There was no time for chatter, and no one noticed a bunch of animals leaving a glass coach. They were all eager to locate some information about the Hugglett spoon or even find the treasure chest.

Molly stood there, with Yo-Yo and Wibbly by her side. She was slightly concerned about splitting everyone up, but Gertrude had flown ahead, and Harry was already trotting round the town, following instructions.

"Slobbers, Gingers see you in a bit," said Molly as they all went their separate ways.

Chapter 9

The plot thickens.

The poem worried Molly a bit as she and the two dogs by her side made their way up the hill towards the ridge, where Robin and Rudge lived. Gertrude appeared and clucked which confirmed that they were expected as she hovered over and then flew to check on the others.

Molly couldn't get the line out of her head, "**Death is imminent for a friend and not foe.**" She'd told Slobbers that the bug dog being killed had nothing to do with this riddle. There was no point in pretending otherwise. She knew it was going to be one of her family, which was now a large family indeed. They got to the ridge where Robin and Rudge sat on their markers waiting to meet the Magical Molly.

Back in the town, Slobbers and the Ginger twins were in and out of the houses and the streets. It was easier than they'd thought as everyone was in a party mood. All had their front doors open and there was a carnival atmosphere in the whole town. They hadn't come across anything exciting to date as Gertrude clucked overhead to check on them.

Harry was trotting round the town and ventured away from the activities and noticed several horses patiently waiting for their owners from competing. They didn't look like competition horses, and he decided to alert Gertrude.

Gertrude clucked and understood his comments and went to find the cats. Slobbers and the twins went to investigate as the two hours were up.

Molly and Wibbly with Yo-Yo curled up in a ball under Wibbly's chest were listening to the kites' chatter. They were magnificent birds, quite large, which had frightened Yo-Yo initially, so he'd hidden. They were indeed looking very regal with their chestnut plumage all plumped out. They were as confused as Molly, but they were also agitated as they were spelled to the Cambrian Mountains and couldn't fly away to help.

"We're sorry we can't be more helpful Molly," sighed Robin.

"We'll have to ask around for you especially as the lady in the lake seems to have us in her radar," suggested Rudge. *"We'll let you know through the Owls of Geraintus if we hear anything. Leave a copy of the riddle with us."*

"I'll leave you my double pin, we can track you on our hovel if you've news," said Molly. She was trying not to sound disheartened as she placed the double pin to Robin's plumage.

"Squawk."

"Come on Molly, we need to go," said Wibbly, equally feeling despondent as Yo-Yo stayed in his chest pocket. Gertrude had reminded them that time was of the essence, and they needed to get back to Harry's cart.

In the meantime, Slobbers and the Ginger twins were inspecting the area where the working horses were all patiently waiting for their owners to return from the competition. Slobbers observed several horses tied up as the Ginger twins went through each aisle checking for something unusual. There was a cart full of coal with the horse sleeping standing up, the next horse was sleeping, and his cart had a lot of household stuff strewn on it. There were obviously several horses carrying goods for their masters.

They didn't notice in their haste the little grubby boy holding a silver and blue silk cloth. He was climbing onto the back of the cart with the household belongings. They didn't notice the treasure chest as it was covered with a thick carpet blanket. The three cats left the area and made their way to Harry's cart.

Everyone was in the trap as Molly decided not to wait for the coach. She was exasperated and needed to get back to the cave and work on the riddle.

"I'm going to fly us back by moonbeam everyone, hold on whilst I administer the spell."

She felt quite fed up and needed to concentrate on this spell as the sooner they got back to the cave, the better they would all feel. Before anyone could ask her what she meant by moonbeam, she'd already started chanting,

"Hedfan, ychell/ headvan ugh-ghell," she repeated three times casting a sprinkle of angel dust over the whole cart by her big bushy tail. Slobbers gasped in

astonishment as did the others, who were all wide-eyed and looked at Molly in awe. The cart attached to Harry was floating through the clouds with Molly murmuring a continuance spell over Harry's head.

Within minutes they floated at great speed towards Saundersfoot as Molly tried to slow it down as they careered and crashed into the Golden Coracle, which was still parked on the beach.

The Coracle twitched with the sudden arrival of a heap of animals. The electric shock went straight to Molly's red collar which made her bolt away from the mountain of furry animals and land on her paws, a few yards away. She looked up straight into Ivor Llewellyn's eyes who looked quite perplexed at the scene in front of him. Garibaldi hearing the commotion had run towards them immediately.

"Sorry, Ivor, forgot the last bit of the spell, but it did get us back tho,'" she grinned. Then she started to whimper as the red collar took hold of her neck, trying to strangle her. As this was happening, the coracle become agitated and decided to attempt to unhinge itself from the padlocked pole.

"Look, the coracle hasn't moved until now Ivor, we must get her inside. Now Molly's back we can move her right away," said Garibaldi beginning to wonder that something else was going on but couldn't put his finger on it right there and then.

"Someone help me get this collar from Molly's neck, it's strangling her," said Wibbly as Yo-Yo used his smaller paw to get around her neck and the collar.

"Rip it off, look she's going into a daze," shouted Slobbers quite anxious. She was very magical. Slobbers as did the others all realised; they needed her more than they'd envisaged.

*"Something isn't right Ivor. We need to get the coracle inside **right away**,"* said Garibaldi. The collar snapped away from Garibaldi's hand and danced in the air, agitating the coracle even more as everyone moved slightly away from it. The Coracle started attacking the pole as the collar circled over it three times as if saying something and flew down the beach and disappeared.

Before anyone moved a muscle to retrieve it, a loud wail was heard from the cave. Bedivere looked at Ivor, who immediately marched to the cave, all the animals followed him. Garibaldi stood looking at the coracle as it subsided and lay still again. He double secured the chain to the pole, muttered he would move it as soon as they'd worked out what commotion was coming from the cave.

Elijas was running from the cave as everyone was approaching him. Garibaldi had caught up and then he realised the noise was coming from one of their secret passages.

"Those passages are locked, whatever is it?" he said aloud and then Wibbly Alf barked furiously and started panting, trying to get his words out quickly. Slobbers

and the two cats decided they needed to take charge and went ahead as Elijas was now as pale as the sand.

"I know who it is," he shouted. *"She might be with the enemy; we must be careful. How she got in there, is really our concern,"* said Wibbly not making sense at all to anyone.

The wailing continued from inside and it was apparent it was a wounded dog or a dog needing to make contact, they needed to act fast.

However, Garibaldi knew instinctively who was in there as he strode ahead with the cats; they had to open the passage door. Molly quickly recovering from being strangled by a red collar went ahead with them.

They all piled into the house and then no one could remember the code for the secret passageway. Frustrated by the lack of urgency with the wizards, Molly moved to the cave door and started muttering a spell, swishing, and scattering angel dust from her tail.

"Agor ydrws, willieannie grigolo/ Ahcohr eh droos, williannie greegoloh"

She swished her tail three times, repeating the spell, the wailing inside continued and suddenly the door exploded, and everyone got covered in sand particles and bricks. The wizards spluttered swaying their cloaks to disperse the cloud of dust. Garibaldi rushed inside the passageway with Molly and dragged out a bloody and wounded retriever. She was in a coma and her fur was torn in numerous places, blood everywhere. Her ear was ripped and there was a hole in her side. Her paw was burnt and close to being ripped from her ankle.

"Quick, we need to examine her," said Molly as she gave Slobbers and Gertrude a command with her tail.

Immediately Slobbers and the ginger twins went outside with Gertrude as there was no one patrolling the beach keeping an eye on the Golden Coracle.

Bedivere fetched the potion tins as Garibaldi started checking her over. Wibbly Alf went and sat at the front door and observed. Elijas repaired the passageway door, and Ivor went to secure the hovel and check for any movements in the kingdom.

Molly suggested a magical brew from Garibaldi as he went to make one in his special teapot. Bedivere was deft and the foul-smelling repair potion was now lingering round the cave, waking the wizards from their passive behaviour. Suddenly everyone was working at top speed as if repairing this dog was crucial to their treasure hunting.

"It's gone, it's gone, it's gone........."

Slobbers swung the front door open shouting in despair as Garibaldi stopped what he was doing and ran out of the cave with Ivor, hot on his heels. Molly stayed with the dog, knowing exactly what had gone. It was inevitable, the wizards had failed to move the coracle all weekend and now it had been taken from under their noses. This dog had been a perfect decoy.

She finished administering the potion as she felt her neck, which was still swollen. Whoever had done this as she recognised the wounds were like Slobbers, she knew that the enemy were far too organised and ahead of them. It was obvious, the sooner they found the spoon and seek some answers the sooner those wizards would get their spells back. In the meantime, Molly moved the dog to the hearth, with Wibbly's help.

"Sit with her Wibbly, she won't be fit for a while, but she'll live."

Molly knew she needed to get the riddle dissected, and now they had the coracle to retrieve along with finding the spoon. The treasure hunt wasn't going to be that straight forward after all.

Chapter 10

Geraintus.

Everyone felt responsible for what had just occurred, especially Ivor Ap Llewellyn. He'd muttered his horror of losing the Coracle and had disappeared to his quarters to lick his wounds. It was pointless to state the obvious. All Molly could think about was the riddle and without the wizards' historical knowledge, she would have to rely on her instincts, Garibaldi's wise information and the animals around her.

The most frightening thought was that the red collar, which was meant to be the most magical collar, had turned nasty towards her. Merlin had informed Molly that this red collar was the most magical of all for the Llewellyn family. She wasn't the right family member who should be wearing it. She wondered who that would be, but until then she had Wibbly bury it, in the sand dunes away from the cave. Millie stirred as she watched Wibbly licking her paws and comforting her.

Garibaldi came in with some tea and she nodded and went to join him at the table. Gertrude had been sent to fly up the secret passageway to see if she could ascertain what had happened. Everyone else had disappeared outside as the security had lapsed. It was too late as the Coracle had been taken. No one had noticed that Yo-Yo had gone on his own mission earlier and hadn't yet returned.

"They should all be back in a bit Molly. We'll have a proper meeting to discuss what we should do from here," said Garibaldi sensing Molly's exasperation and loss. He felt the same.

"Any news, via the hovel?"

"No, no movements as such. Ivor is taking it badly. I gave him a sleeping-draught. I shall get him up when the others arrive."

Rat-tat-tat.

The door opened as Wibbly rushed over to make sure as Elijas, Bedivere and Geraintus walked in.

"I'll go and get Ivor," said Garibaldi as the wizards and Geraintus made themselves comfortable around the table. They were silent and it was apparent that the coracle being taken earlier had had a damaging effect on them all. Not least Ivor who appeared bedraggled and needing even more sleep than the sleep induced coma he'd been given.

"How's the dog?" asked Elijas, who felt that this whole family were losing the plot, even more so than before.

"Her name is Millie and she's going to recover. However, it could take a while. She was heavily attacked and beaten, left for dead, I presume," said Garibaldi, who knew all about her but didn't elaborate. He knew that

Molly had already sussed her out, she was incredible the aura of knowledge she was giving him on occasions.

"Let's discuss where we're going from here. I suggest we don't leave this cave until we have a plan," said Molly as they all looked at the completed puzzle on the table.

"The map is quite self-explanatory," said Bedivere as they all glanced at the puzzle. *"The castles in Carmarthenshire are all marked in navy blue. I didn't realise there was so many."*

"Yes, but Manorbier is missing," said Molly." *There are too many here to visit, there must be over a dozen in this county let alone Pembrokeshire."*

"How many castles in this area, which have direct Llewellyn descendants living in them?" asked Elijas, who didn't know all the family and needed this family to get on with proceedings. They were taking forever in his opinion.

"Apart from Carew, Coch and Cardiff, as they are unoccupied, all of them," answered Bedivere.

"We, as the Llewellyn family have the right to live in any castle and the occupants, although descendants would have to leave. For example, if Molly wanted to live in Caernarvon."

"Tudor's already part of this family and lives there, I would certainly not throw him out. We're wasting time, I'll live in one of these unoccupied ones that will save arguments later. Let's concentrate on this riddle and see what we can decipher from the puzzle and the poem," said Molly not wishing to be side-tracked anymore.

"Yes, he may live in Caernarvon Castle, so why is it circled on this puzzle, look?" said Ivor peering closer than the others. They all looked, and silence ensued round the table for a moment.

"It's to throw us off the scent. We thought he was a traitor, but in fact, he's family. I don't believe we need to make much of this," said Elijas.

"Then why did this dog go with Bethesda, our staunch enemy to spy on Tudor at the Castle?" asked Molly.

"Good point," said Bedivere as Elijas went slightly crimson in colour being challenged by the Magical Molly.

"I know," said Garibaldi timing his knowledge to inform Molly and the others.

"Millie is a Llewellyn dog, she was lost from us in a previous battle because the enemy witnessed her powers through her magical paw, they kept her as their own. She's been found out, attacked and she's made her way back to us, her rightful owners. She may have something to tell us?"

"Gertrude will verify this as she is in the tunnel as we speak," said Molly looking at the bedraggled sick dog on the hearth. Her family of creatures was indeed growing. The sooner she found this treasure, the quicker everyone could get on with their lives.

"I can also verify she wasn't on the hovel at all. Kester flew around the castle like a demented bat, looking for

her. She never made it inside the grounds of the castle. I'm surprised Bethesda hasn't knocked on our door as he's missing his dog."

"Maybe Bethesda isn't happy about not finding something at Tudors as we saw him going through his papers in the middle of the night. The Croggs are looking for something. They're looking for this puzzle. Remember Tudor found it by mistake after that attack. There's something obvious on this puzzle and we need to find it," said Molly.

This statement made them all concentrate hard on the puzzle on the table and Garibaldi interrupted them, with a fresh brew.

"I'm going to summon Tudor to ask him, what do you all think?"

"I'm not sure," said Molly.

"Why not?" asked Ivor knowing full well the answer.

"The riddle didn't mention if the friend to be killed was family or foe. We're not sure which camp he's in."

"Molly, this is precisely why we need to tackle him. It would be good to see his reaction to the dog on the hearth, as he should know who she is. He knows the family history as well as me and Garibaldi," said Ivor taking command.

"Very well, you've got a point. Also, he's to stand to lose a castle too if the Croggs find the treasure first. I may be a little hasty in judging him," said Molly graciously this riddle playing on her mind.

"This isn't getting us anywhere, let's look at this poem once again, while Gari sends for Tudor," said Bedivere.

Tap, tap, tap.

Tudor in full colourful robes entered the room, with his bat hanging from his long-sleeved cloak as he sauntered into the living room.

"Oh goodness gracious me! Why have you got Millie here, what's happened?"

There was silence as everyone in advance of Tudor arriving had agreed to wait for information from Tudor himself. They needed to be reassured that he was on their side. They also decided not to mention the stolen Coracle; in fact, no one was to give away any information unless it was necessary.

Molly spoke, *"We're hoping you could enlighten us Tudor on Bethesda's visit and now this,"* as she waved her paw towards the comatose retriever.

"I've no idea what's going on," exclaimed Tudor as he went to the dog on the hearth and nodded feeling her weak pulse.

"All I know is that Bethesda came to a meeting about the imminent singing festival, which they want to hold in my castle grounds again, this year. There's nothing funny about that, mind you I did wonder where his dog was. I did ask him where Millie was over dinner, and he assumed she was outside with the black labs in the inner courtyard. What's happened? You all obviously want an

explanation," said Tudor, as he looked round the table. Garibaldi wasn't happy with this situation, picked up the teapot and went to make a fresh brew.

"Kester mentioned after Bethesda's visit that he'd spotted Bethesda going through all my paperwork. There's nothing incriminating in my castle, we all know where we keep our papers. I'm as much concerned about this as you are. I suppose you were going to tell me that you'd lost the coracle or were you going to keep that from me. We're all family, I'm on your side, you know. Why don't you all tell me what you make of this puzzle now that you've finished it? When Millie wakes up, she'll be able to give us more information on the Croggs," said Tudor finally sitting down. Everyone visibly relaxed with Garibaldi returning red in the face looking a bit foolish for doubting him.

Molly was reassured and started to give him the information which reflected they'd read the finished puzzle. They read the riddle again, more for Tudors' benefit this time, but the more they read it, the more worried Molly quietly became.

"Death is imminent for a friend and not foe, Use your magical, mystical power and mystical spell. Eagles are coming; red kites or bats; no. Find the clue, an ancient place with wishing well.

Purple is strong, but there is turquoise blue. Not to paddle, but carry, Coracle Gold. Nesta, Helen of Wales, says it's true. Treasure chest needs to be found and sold. Magical, Mystical Molly, it's written

in the mud. You and your friends mustn't shed the first blood!"

"*Gosh*," said Tudor, "*There're loads of clues here, where are we on a plan? Do we know how close the Croggs are in finding the spoon, anyone?*"

Garibaldi interrupted.

"*Gertrude is flying back over the beach,*" as he returned from the parlour checking the hovel. "*Yo-Yo is trotting beneath her; he went on a mission of his own. Let's see what they have to say and then we need to finish deciphering the map as Tudor's right, we need to be getting on with it.*"

The door slammed open, Slobbers and Wibbly Alf letting them in. Gertrude squawked in clucking non-stop, and she flew straight to the coracle chair and flopped on it very animated. Yo-Yo sat next to the chair and waited his turn to relay what he'd gathered.

Molly, astute as ever started the questions to Gertrude.

"*What did you find in the passageway and where does it lead to?*

"*Cluck, the passageway goes all the way to Harlech Castle.*"

A shock wave of horror from the rest of the family as she continued with Ivor studying the map, looking for Harlech Castle on the puzzle.

"*It's on here,*" said Ivor aloud.

"*Let Gertrude finish Ivor and then we'll talk about it,*" said Molly eager to get on and hear everything.

"*Cluck, cluck, cluck. The passageway is covered with scorch marks from the entrance to Harlech; the scorch marks resemble the marks on Slobbers when he got attacked and the ones on Millie.*"

"*I know who they belong to,*" shouted Yo-Yo as he wanted to tell them what he'd found and quickly Molly realised they were on to something.

"*Well done, Gertrude,*" said Garibaldi as the wizards nodded.

Wibbly Alf on the nod from Yo-You went to fetch something from outside the front door. He carried a mass of green in his mouth and dropped it at Yo-Yo's feet. Wibbly went back to the front door, which he guarded, and his link chain jangled quietly every time he moved and swished his tail.

"*I went to Laugharne after Slobbers told us his tale and on the banks of the beach, there are these. They're hidden from sight but have been dug out ready for something,*" said Yo-Yo as Garibaldi smiled at Molly. She had everything covered even though she hadn't said where Yo- Yo had gone.

"*Let's look at them,*" said Tudor getting up and examining the green moss net.

"*It's the same shape as those Beggly creatures that attacked Slobbers,*" said Molly immediately as Tudor had it held up. The distinctive oval shaped netting was evident the same size as those creatures.

"Oh no, the Begglys are dreadful creatures," commented Elijas gravely, who'd been silent up to now.

"What do you know about them, Elijas?" asked Molly.

"Bedivere knows more than me," he retorted.

"They're oval shaped and have a shimmer type leather skin like a beetle creature. They don't speak but have a three antennae system that connects with the instructions they're given. They attack via those antennae and if hit the person or animal will be left scorched, maimed, or killed."

"How do you know so much about the enemy's creatures Bedivere?" queried Tudor.

"You should always know your enemies Tudor, even if you don't wish to tackle them. You ought to know what they're capable of in combat," replied Bedivere not happy to be challenged on these creatures.

"Ok gentlemen, Yo-Yo, you've done a grand job. We need to be aware that they're here," said Molly. *"They're spying on us as we speak. Yo-Yo join Millie by the hearth, we need your strength passed to her, as we need her better. We must assume we're being always watched."*

Yo-Yo curled up in a ball of fluff and with his usual trick rolled towards Millie and tucked himself under her tummy as she heaved a sigh, recognising his presence.

"According to the hovel, there are no creatures anywhere near us right now," said Garibaldi having checked from hearing about the Beggly creature.

"Let's get on with this list then," said Geraintus who up until that moment hadn't contributed any ideas. His little notebook with parchment was already out on the table and he'd started making notes.

"Harlech Castle is Owain's. He's our distant cousin and mentioned by Gertrude is on the list along with Manorbier Castle, as it's missing."

"Place Caernarvon on the list too," said Bedivere.

"Why my Castle?" said Tudor.

"It's circled for a reason, we don't know what that is yet," said Bedivere.

"Bedivere is right, Tudor, we need to start a list and then eliminate them as we check the poem."

Molly, with her neck still hurting from wearing the red collar, was getting exasperated but knew that this process was going to be slow. She was reliant, as was the other dogs, on the wizards' knowledge. They weren't forthcoming at all unless it was cajoled out of them. Even Garibaldi, who knew all the past historical events, didn't seem to be giving much information either.

Rat tat tat

Wibbly Alf allowed in Slobbers who was wet and needed to speak to Molly.

"I've been swimming with Tom the turtle, Molly. He confirmed that he saw three little people with lots of oval black creatures running up the sand pulling our coracle with silkworm. Just thought I ought to tell you

right away," as he shook his thick fur over everyone. He smiled at his master Garibaldi and went back outside to patrol the beach.

"At least we know it was the Croggs. We still don't know who the others were at Symonds Yat," said Elijas trying to contribute.

"Right, we have some letters missing here, that doesn't fit the other puzzle, these might be clues," said Molly going through them. More importantly ignoring the pertinent comment made by Elijas. Everyone else ignored it too.

"We've made up words from those letters; they are 'Cavern,' 'lady,' and 'night.' The other words are 'river,' 'white' and 'golden,' with three letters left. They're e, a, and l," said Bedivere hoping his puzzle expertise was going to be recognised. Ivor and he had spent the previous night going through the possibilities and these were the words they had made up.

"Lady could mean the lady of the lake," said Molly.

"Yes, she does come out at night," murmured Ivor as Geraintus scribbled everyone's comments in his notebook.

"The three missing letters could spell coracle, but that may be too obvious," said Tudor.

"We need to write it all down, our thoughts, nothing right now is wrong or right," said Molly as they continued.

Geraintus scribbled something of his own on the pad; he would mention this in a minute.

"We need to cross check each castle we have on this checklist against the words and the riddle. We simply can't visit every castle in the kingdom, we haven't got the time. We need to find the spoon, before the Croggs find it and declare it as theirs," said Molly sounding very frustrated.

"Let's have a minute to check the cave," said Ivor seeing frustrations beginning to show.

Geraintus scribbled some more, and the wizards all got up to stretch their legs for a moment. Garibaldi went to make tea and check the hovel as Molly went outside to check on her troops. She came back in and looked at Millie on the hearth and realised Yo-Yo was still under her belly keeping her warm and her breathing was better. Her bandaged paw would soon need a new dressing. Her ripped ear was healing perfectly, and it was evident she was improving, those potions had worked.

"She was wrongly attacked," murmured Molly to Yo-Yo as he fidgeted in his ball state in agreement.

Back to the table, Geraintus had moved to the top and seemed to have rearranged his papers. Geraintus started on his notes and had spent the past hour or so deep in thought. He was an expert in these types of clues.

"*Right, the first line of the riddle, states someone is going to die, there's no clue there it's a riddle fact, I'll call it.*"

Before anyone could comment on his attitude, he continued,

"*The next line is telling us that Molly must always use her magical capabilities to save us. The third line is for your thought's wizards, its **'eagles are coming; red kites or bats; no'**"*

"*This could mean Robin and Rudge as they are red kites. Our own bats are Drool at Harlech and Tudors Kester, we don't know any eagles,*" said Geraintus, "*Any ideas anyone?*"

"*Are these Eagles coming to harm us or are they friendly?*" asked Garibaldi confused trying to rack his brains on this line.

"*No idea, but Geraintus write it down,*" said Molly, continuing to the next line.

"*The next two lines are about our coloured collars and robes and the coracle mustn't be placed in water. The Croggs are going to have a surprise if they plan to float it to a hiding place.*"

A chuckle went around the table for a moment as Geraintus continued,

"*Nesta, Helen of Wales says it's true.*"

"*Nesta, bless her lives in Carew Castle and she mumbles about things. Whether they're true is a matter of opinion. Carew must go on the list. She's also known as* the Lady in White," said Ivor realising that was one clue with an answer."

"The rest of the riddle talks about not shedding the first blood."

"Does that mean I can't kill first if any of you are in danger?" asked Molly wanting a straight answer.

Ivor fidgeted in his chair and was rescued by Tudor.

"Millie is family, she's been attacked already, therefore, whoever attacks us from today, we as a family have agreed that we haven't attacked first."

"The mud could be a clue too," said Garibaldi.

A green pebble plopped inside the door via Slobbers.

"Tudor, your castle has sent a pebble, do you want to read it?" asked Garibaldi as he fetched it from Wibbly.

"Yes, it might be information on our Millie. This is interesting," said Tudor as Garibaldi interrupted him.

"There's movement with those three dots on the hovel. They're heading towards Carew castle, that area. We need to intercept them or put some spies in place quickly."

Ignoring Gari's comment, Tudor continued, *"This helps our poem. Drool, Owain's bat, can confirm that Millie was attacked outside Caernarvon Castle unbeknown to Bethesda. He states that she was killed and thrown over the cliff edge. They've no idea how she got into the passageway which is linked to my Castle."*

"*Look she's stirring,*" said Wibbly from the front door.

They all looked at Millie and Yo-Yo curled away from her as she lifted her head slowly from the floor.

"*I found the old entrance to Caernarvon passage, spelled it open with my paw and crawled in, but two of those creatures followed me and attacked me inside, blowing up my paw, leaving me for dead. I just crawled to the end knowing the path had changed to the cave,*" as Millie's head fell back on the floor, and she went to sleep exhausted. Yo-Yo rolled back round to her tummy to comfort her.

"*How did you know that I'd changed the passages?*" asked Tudor, who couldn't see her from where he sat at the table and was curious.

"*She's gone back to sleep Tudor, that question can wait. She is your magical dog; she'll be an asset to us. I don't think we need to question her integrity or loyalty. Let's move back to this puzzle, we have enemy moving, we think. We need to decide what we should do first.*"

"*Molly's right, as the bats have been mentioned and we need more of a structured in-flight communication system, why don't we bring my whispering fig tree over here? We can get my owls and the kites, when they have information to send the detail to the fig tree which will whisper the contents of any pebbles or messages directly to us, via Gertrude,*" suggested Geraintus. "*At least that would help keep us abreast on any extra activity going on, if the hovel misses it or we miss it ourselves.*"

"*How could the fig tree help us Geraintus?*" asked Molly who didn't know anything about this whispering fig tree until that moment.

"*Drool and Kester send messages to the tree, the highest in the area. The tree protected me from near cremation last year as bandits set my house on fire. The tree was able to send a message in advance via the bats to warn me. This tree could link up with Robin and Rudge easily and Gertrude could gather the information.*"

"*How do we link up to the tree?*"

"*We use your spells to make it mystical and tune in to our network, it won't take long.*"

"*Sounds like a plan Geraintus, we'll fetch it later today. In the meantime, let's get some idea on what else we need to action with our clues,*" said Molly thinking this was a clever idea but she still wanted another plan in place.

"*There someone else moving towards Cardigan, I think it's the treasure chest, it's coming from Tregaron, as we might have missed it. We have two problems now,*" said Garibaldi as he proceeded to pour tea round the table as the wizards became exasperated. Lunch was a quiet affair as they needed a plan and Molly and Slobbers with Geraintus needed to depart to collect the whispering fig tree.

***

Somewhere in Tregaron the Romani family were making their way out of the Town, whilst everyone was sleeping. Their horse and cart were laden with belongings and the young lad held on tight with his Mum, amongst the family belongings. They were heading for the ferry at Pembroke, as the head of the family had secured work in Ireland, and they were on their way to meet it.

Chapter 11

The Croggs of St Clears celebrate.

The chapel hall in St. Clears was a mass of supporters all celebrating the easy capture of the Golden Coracle. The hall was crammed to standing room only with little people patiently waiting for the arrival of the first Crogg of St. Clears, Kentav Crogg. He, along with his two brothers were gathering massive support for the quest of being the First Family of Wales.

On the platform in front of the little people, was a table with parchments of paper. To the side of the parchments, was Zupp, head bug dog and known to all enemy factions as the Beggly creature.

The place erupted as the three brothers with Bethesda following them arrived. They made their way through the crowds to the platform, where Blodwen had provided chairs in advance at the table. Bethesda for some reason was secretly glad he hadn't been a part of the Golden Coracle capture. He didn't know why but he had a sense of unease at that moment, and he was beginning to feel uncomfortable amongst the Croggs.

Kentav, bursting with confidence and authority stood at the table as everyone sat. Zupp moved to his side as Ali stomped his stick on the floor for silence.

131

"Thanks everyone, we're delighted with your support. We've captured the coracle and....."

Another eruption of shouting and cheer went up in the hall.

"Shhhh everyone, please," shouted Trent. However, he was also amazed that his brother had pulled it off.

"Right, to fill you all in on where we're up to on the quest of retrieving what is actually ours...."

Another roar of delight from the crowd.

"Shh......" shouted Trent, *"Let the man speak."*

"First of all, this is Zupp everyone. He'll tell you what's happened on his mission."

"We've succeeded in killing the Llewellyn dog Millie, whilst they were organising a singing event at Caernarvon Castle. Bethesda was good cover, and she is no longer with us. We need to eliminate all potential threat to the Crogg mission in winning back the treasure......."

The Beggly three antennae was spinning round the room on the oval body of the bug dog as Bethesda felt quite faint as he heard this news. He tried to compose himself and had to pretend he was pleased. There was something wrong here. He knew that the Beggly creatures and his pack, were deadly and the only one able to communicate with humans was Zupp. The rest of them received instructions via Zupp and attacked until they were killed themselves. They had no lock down mechanism or a stop button. They were automated and followed the first instruction. They were self-multiplying on a farm close to Kentav's Hutlet and Bethesda suddenly went cold with fear. His thoughts were interrupted as the crowd started throwing their hats in the air for a moment.

"Yes, we shall take the coracle to Aberaeron in the morning. Currently, it's hiding in a secret place. We don't want any of you slipping up in the pub and giving the game away," smiled Kentav knowing the less they knew the better it was for him.

"Where are you hiding the coracle?" asked an astute little person in the front row.

"We're not going to give out the destination. We shall go to Aberaeron first as the Beggly army are gathering there, in readiness for the next mission. Our cousin, Islwyn, who runs the honey ice-cream factory, will be instrumental in giving us the low down on what's been going down with the Llewellyn family."

A cheer went up from the crowd.

"I want to thank you all for your help to make more Coracles; we're now ready to get the Hugglett spoon from the Llewellyn family. Soon we will live in Cardiff castle. 'Till next week folks..."

The euphoria of the supporters continued and spilled over into the adjacent pub as Kentav with his brothers went up the hill to his hutlet for a private meeting. Bethesda, unhappy followed suit wishing Jethro his brother, the Undertaker wasn't so busy burying little people this evening, to support him.

Blodwen bursting with pride was already home and had prepared a feast to celebrate her husband's newfound popularity and success.

Bethesda couldn't contain himself any longer and as soon as they were all sat, he asked the question. *"Why did the Begglys kill Millie, Kentav? What made them think she was a liability?"*

"I don't know why you were so fond of that dog Bethesda; you knew she wasn't ours in the first place. The Begglys saw her contact Drool or Kester and thought she was going to relay the plan of the coracle hijack to them, so they killed her. It's no big deal she was a liability for that reason," said Kentav tucking into one of Blodwen's big ham sandwiches and slurping his mug of tea.

Bethesda kept a straight face and shoved a sandwich in his mouth to keep himself from saying something he might regret. He wasn't happy and needed to get this meeting done, to get back and speak to Jethro.

"Let's eat, Ali what's the next stage of our plan?" said Kentav full of himself and enjoying the control he felt right at that time.

"Yes, why are we really going to Aberaeron, Kentav? It seems out of the way a bit?" asked Bethesda needing to know the whole plan suddenly.

"We do need to collect the Beggly army who are ready for us to challenge the Llewellyn's' for the spoon. We will go via Cardigan just in case we're being watched

or followed. By the time we reach Aberaeron the Begglys will be ready to annihilate the whole lot of them."

Bethesda found it increasingly difficult to keep his face from showing horror as he wasn't aware, they were going to kill the whole family to retain the first family of Wales's title.

Kentav, confident with his idea, didn't notice Bethesda quietly going white with anguish as he continued,

"Once we've obliterated the enemy and I'm surprised we haven't seen the wizards turn up, like last time. Anyway, we will take the coracle to Manorbier Castle as Trent's girlfriend, Katrin has moved into the castle. This is perfect to hide the coracle and it's on Ivor Ap Llewellyn's doorstep and the last place he would think to look for it, it's perfect for that reason alone."

"I didn't know you had a girlfriend who lives in a Llewellyn castle," frowned Ali.

"Her father has been given the castle as a thank you for all his work for the Croggs abroad and Geraldus Ap Llewellyn, the knight, has allowed them to live in it for the time being. Until their home is ready in Tenby, they're building a new hutlet there," explained Trent a bit uneasy. He knew more and this wasn't the right time to tell anyone about his relationship with Katrin.

"Why don't we go straight there and then sort out the army, as it seems as if we're going back on ourselves," said Bethesda.

"There's method in my madness Bethesda. We need to collect the army; we need them in case that Magical Molly turns up with her wizards. We mustn't underestimate them, even if we haven't seen them yet," said Kentav a bit worried that the wizards hadn't been round his hutlet creating havoc. This was very unusual.

"We've prepared the beach areas for when we go to see Ivor demanding where the spoon is, we're ready. We just need to get the coracle hidden and we're there. It shouldn't take us long, a few days, if we leave at dawn or dusk, which would be better than full daylight. We need to get prepared to leave at once."

"We have spies on Saundersfoot beach all the time and they're reporting to Zupp. He is patrolling our hutlets and so far, there's no movement. We three brothers shall leave at first light with the coracle."

Trent looked surprised to be included in this.

"Don't look so surprised Trent. You may be stupid at times, but we're brothers, and we shall take the treasures together and win the castles together. I'm going to live in Cardiff Castle, I've already decided," smiled Kentav as Bethesda got up to leave.

"I shall come over first thing Kentav, to see you off in one piece. I bid you all good night. Congratulations to you all."

Bethesda quietly skimmed down the hill and couldn't wait to get home, he had a lot of thinking to do, and he needed to speak to Jethro. He was very unhappy with this situation. He was sad about Millie. He was the man of the cloth, and no one had told him there would be murder and killings.

Bethesda was awake all night. He knew Blodwen would need someone to help her in the carpentry business and he also knew that he couldn't live with people who had no disregard for each other or the magical creatures that were around them. He decided and would tell Jethro, once the Croggs had left with the coracle.

Dawn came quickly and the Croggs were outside the carpentry business with a few of their staunch supporters gathering, to see them off.

Bethesda and Kentav came out of the factory and Kentav shook Bethesda's hands, thanking him for offering to stay, to assist his wife with the business. Kentav was so preoccupied with this mission, he wouldn't have noticed if Bethesda hadn't suggested this perfect cover of his. There were two coracles outside the factory, and this confused Bethesda immediately.

"Why have you two coracles, Trent?"

"One is for provisions and blankets and a decoy just in case we need it. Kentav has thought of everything," said Trent also a bit uncomfortable but not sure why at that point in time.

"It does make sense Trent," retorted Ali as he came back from giving Zupp his instructions. The Beggly creature zipped back and forth in front of them and behind them checking for any persons, who could be enemy. He was very efficient, his antennae spinning like

radar and his shiny pearlescent body was glimmering in the early light, dazzling anyone looking straight at him.

"Good luck, good luck" ... the cheer went up as the supporters wished the Croggs on their way. The journey had commenced to hide the coracle.

Back at Bethesda's hut, there was a heated argument going on between Jethro and Bethesda in the front room.

"But they're giving me all their orders Bethesda. They're good for my business; he was always able to make me cheap coffins for all the poor families. I know his attitude annoys me too, but we we're making good money from them."

"It's not the money Jethro," said Bethesda. *"I know he contributed a lot to my chapel charities and helped us all, but he is an evil, conniving man and I can see bloodshed. I don't want to be a part of it Jethro, I'm done. He got Millie killed and you know how I feel about that."*

"Have you checked her things? If we leave and defect, surely, we'd better ask Ivor Ap Llewellyn for an audience as you know they scare me," said Jethro. His one black eye rolled round in his head and the other green one looked a bit startled.

"They may not accept us as friends as we have lived with the enemy for over ten years. We may find ourselves ostracised without any family if we're not careful," said Jethro as Bethesda was looking in Millie's basket.

"Look Jethro, what's this, look... here in her basket."

Inside the basket was several collars littered about and a few blankets all an assortment of colours.

"I didn't realise she had so many collars, I didn't pay much attention to her obviously, Jethro."

"What's this?"

Under the basket lining, was a turquoise blue cloth with hundreds of silver moons scattered over it. They started dancing as Jethro held it up for them both to inspect.

"Oh my, we must take this back to Ivor Ap Llewellyn," Bethesda said as soon as the moons started to react. *"We shall send them a red pebble, asking for an audience and to take Millie's belongings back to the rightful owner. We need to defect Jethro, at once. This is part of the Llewellyn's crest look; the turquoise and purple colours are also twinkling."*

"This could be our peace offering as such Bethesda. Go and write that pebble immediately."

"What do you think to this Jethro?" asked Bethesda knowing this was the most important pebble he'd ever written.

"In memory of our Millie, we're defecting and unhappy with the future situation. Have contents of Millie's basket, which will be of urgent interest. An invitation to explain ourselves would benefit and please us all. Bethesda and Jethro."

The plan was set; they would leave in the morning for Manorbier where their sister lived. They both had professions that could be administered anywhere. It was more necessary to go, regardless of the response from the pebble to Ivor Ap Llewellyn. Blodwen had accepted Bethesda's excuse for needing to visit his sister, who wasn't well. She was more than capable of running the business without Kentav and she didn't need Bethesda interfering. They were ready; they needed to wait for the pebble to return, hopefully before their coach first thing...

***

The Croggs were making real progress with Kentav leading the way, pleased as he had another plan. A plan, he hadn't yet told his brothers. Trent was behind Kentav with the second coracle with Ali, pleased that Kentav had found his idea a good one. Ali was suspicious of the whole thing but decided to watch his brothers like a hawk. They were all pleased however as to date, there had been no sign of the enemy.

***

In the middle of the night, the pebble arrived by special goose as Garibaldi responded, not waking anyone from their sleep. It had been a long few days and this news was certainly interesting. Millie's collar, as she continued to lay by the hearth with Yo-Yo snuggled to her, was awake too, the turquoise stones responding to Gari's pebble scribbling. He knew all about it and smiled. It was time for Millie to return to their family. Ivor would have a fit when he realised that two Croggs had requested a meeting. That could wait until morning. It was time to rest, there was trouble ahead he could feel it. The hovel was showing movement from St. Clears, another problem. He would stay up and keep an eye on it.

Chapter 12

The whispering fig tree.

Molly was in Garibaldi's shed at the bottom of Ivor's Garden. She was finalising the security detail around the wizards. She was also deciding on who was coming with her to escort the tree to the cave. Ginger One was sitting above the shed, just in case. Wibbly Alf sat outside the cave entrance, keeping watch.

"It's too risky. All the way to Pendine and back without an escort, some of us will need to come with you."

"I'll be better off on my own as no-one will be looking out for me. They'll expect me to have an escort that's my point," stated Molly exasperated. They all wanted to go with her, but the cave and wizards needed protection.

"Someone needs to be with Millie. She has in fact been attacked, so the enemy have already shed first blood," said Yo-Yo. *"Maybe she was attacked as a message, some of us will need to stay, Molly's right."*

Molly made a snap decision otherwise it would be nightfall before the simple task was done.

"Wibbly, stay here and look after Millie. Gertrude, Slobbers and Yo-Yo you come with me. Gertrude needs to familiarize herself immediately with the tree as she'll be the chief message taker once it's planted here."

Everyone nodded in agreement.

"Ginger One and Two with Harry patrol the beaches and pebble Gertrude if there's anything suspicious. If that's the case, we'll come straight back."

"Right, we'll go in a moment. I must emphasise, we must make sure the wizards stay indoors, whilst we're away. They're losing their powers fast. Wibbly make sure they stay inside, won't you?"

"Yes Molly. Can you see that my link chain's been making funny twinkling noises ever since Millie's arrived? Do you know what that could mean?"

"It means there's something spooky going on," said Yo-Yo trying to sound braver than he felt. He had a funny feeling that things were about to get tricky.

"I hadn't noticed Wibbly, and I should have. Whatever does this mean?"

"It means that Millie is more Llewellyn than we thought, and Garibaldi will be the one to tell us more once we get back. We just need to ask him. The spoon is trying to contact Millie, through her collar and Wibbly through his chain," said Slobbers as he knew something.

"There's an element of sense in that, it's important that Wibbly and Millie stay here until we get back. Ok, let's go everyone," said Molly happy these animals knew a lot and she was grateful for their comments.

They left with Garibaldi having pinned a double pin on each of them, so he could track them on the hovel. He didn't tell Molly about the new movements on the hovel. It was best to let them go, and he'd discuss with Ivor first. They were not going in the same direction, so it was safe not to worry them, but then he thought again.

"Molly, there's another set of movements going towards Cardigan, I'm not sure who they are but you'll need to be always vigilant and hurry back. We should have some answers by then and Ivor and Bedivere will have finalised some plan. Don't worry. Be safe all of you."

Slobbers and Yo-Yo looked alarmed at this news, but Molly took it in her stride and was ready to leave.

"We will go to Pendine and come straight back with the tree. We can tackle the next plan once we've got our messaging system in place. We must go, Geraintus will be wondering where we are."

The animals watched them leave and Garibaldi went indoors to make some more Welsh cakes. That always kept him busy, and he needed to think, what the Croggs were up to now? They were on route here. He started to panic thinking of that and made some tea first. He needed to keep the wizards busy before they started worrying about who was moving around in the county. `

"Gari's right Bedivere. We need to sort this out before they come back," said Ivor trying to concentrate.

"Ivor, why don't you write to all the castles and ask them if they have a wishing well on the grounds of their property, so we can add that castle to the clue list. While you're at it, ask them if they have a cavern on site. Ivor,

have you remembered that Manorbier Castle is missing, as Molly spotted it immediately. Add it on; there could be a reason."

"This list will be too big if you continue with this instruction, Bedivere."

"We need to start somewhere, Ivor. It's best to start them on the list and once we get the information back from everyone, we can eliminate that castle from the list."

"Look, Millie is stirring. I'll fetch Wibbly as he's meant to look out for her," said Bedivere getting up. But Garibaldi was already ahead of him and outside suggesting he started Millie on some recovery exercise to get her stronger.

Ginger One and Two came in and informed the wizards they'd be outside the cave while Wibbly was exercising Millie, and the cave was secure. Every time, Millie and Wibbly were close to each other, their respective collar and chain started talking, it was quite bizarre.

The wizards were deep in conversation with the clues from the words to the riddle as the hovel started hissing like a dozen kettles, all at once. Garibaldi dropped his Welsh cake mixture and ran to the parlour. There was a mass of dots moving from Aberaeron to Cardigan direction, far more than earlier. He could only assume it was the Croggs moving the coracle. They'd gathered their army on route. His heart fell to his stomach; this was going to be a nightmare.

Suddenly the current three dots started moving too and he guessed they were from Tregaron town. They must have the spoon, he thought quickly. They wouldn't be showing up otherwise. The three dots were moving towards the same direction as the mass of dots. Soon their paths would meet before any of the Llewellyn's had a chance to investigate. He could only hope that Molly wasn't long as he daren't send an aging wizard that was losing his faculties. He had to tell them, but he had to pray that Molly would get back in time to deal with it. This was indeed her next task.

***

Molly and her party were not far away from Pendine. They stopped and Molly started giving out instructions.

"Gertrude, fly ahead and make Geraintus aware, we're nearby. We need to see the smoke from his chimney, and then we'll take the shortcut. We need to be quick."

Plop, plop, plop.

"Why is Gari sending us a pebble?" asked Slobbers as he quickly read it.

"What is it?" asked Molly as Gertrude flew towards Geraintus' house.

"We need to complete mission as a matter of urgency. New mission requiring urgent attention."

"Come on, we can't wait for Geraintus to light the fire let's go," said Molly knowing Garibaldi wouldn't be

146

sending out cryptic instructions unless something was wrong at the cave.

They quickened their pace and suddenly the sight of smoke appeared on the skyline which made them move even faster.

"Look Geraintus has lit the fire, follow this trail," urged Molly as Slobbers went ahead and Yo-Yo followed behind. Gertrude flew overhead and clucked and flew towards the smoke as they came to a clearing, like a close. There were miss-shaped looking houses dotted in each corner. In the furthest corner stood a tall crinkly house with three turrets, all higgledy piggely. Geraintus stood on the front step grinning from one green ear to the other. They all ran towards him and went quickly inside with Geraintus ushering them to the back of the house, where the whispering fig tree stood in the middle of the lawn, towering over everything in its vicinity.

"How are we to move this monstrosity?" whispered Yo-Yo to Slobbers.

"By magic Yo-Yo, just you wait and see," said Slobbers also in awe of its size.

The whispering fig tree started to talk immediately and nearly caught Yo-Yo with one of its lower branches as he quickly ducked from its power. The swaying of the branches was creating a strong wind.

"Goodness, Molly how are you going to calm this tree down?"

Geraintus smiled and started to give out instructions.

"Gertrude needs to come in from the front door, Yo-Yo. Can you fetch her? Molly the tree must get to know you, Slobbers and Yo-Yo. You must tell it all about the riddle and all the family. The tree needs to know what we're trying to achieve, and it will give us a clue or tell us how to move it."

"Right, Slobbers climb to the top on the right and I'll go to the left. We have some balance then," said Molly quite excited about using her spells and magic at last. Slobbers started to climb the tree as Geraintus began to soothe the tree by humming at it. Molly arrived at the top and Slobbers was at the opposite end.

Yo-Yo was quite happy to be acknowledged by the tree on the lawn. His collar started to tingle, and he yelped in surprise. The tree began to sway, and Yo-Yo started to feel faint with the collar on his neck agitating furiously as if to strangle him. He yelped again and Geraintus went to save him as Molly was chanting, unable to stop what she was doing. Gertrude was squawking consistently overhead, being involved with Molly's spell.

Gertrude eventually perched on top of the tree and held on, the tree started to respond to Molly's riddle and poor Slobbers felt quite sick. He hadn't told anyone that he feared heights, just because he could swim. Didn't anyone presume he had no weaknesses? He held on; his long silver tail wrapped around the thickest branch for dear life. He scrunched up his eyes and nose, keeping his paws on the branch and hoping he wasn't going to be sick.

Molly was going for the full spell and Slobbers just hoped that the fig tree would get the instruction first time round. Slobbers stuck his head through the branches and nearly fell out of the tree as he watched Geraintus trying to dislodge Yo-Yo's collar. He couldn't get down to help; the tree was swaying so violently. He wondered how Molly could just stand on the branch, her bushy tail in the air, throwing out instructions and riddles. He held on, closed his eyes again and listened to the full force of her spell.

"Caiooiac, caiooiac, ewyllys adar, ewyllys adar, benialli, benialli, Kaheeoh-oyack, Kaheeoh-oyack, ehu-ugh-sheece, ahdahr ,ehu-ugh-sheece, ahdahr, benialli, benialli, whispering fig tree respond," as she continued to repeat this several times followed by the riddle, which she knew word perfect,

"Death is imminent for a friend and not foe, Use your magical, mystical power and spell. Eagles are coming; red kites or bats, no; Find the clue, an ancient place with wishing well, Purple is strong but there is turquoise blue. Not to paddle, but carry, Coracle Gold. Nesta, Helen of Wales says it's true. Treasure chest needs to be found and sold, Magical, Mystical Molly, it's written in the mud. You or your friends mustn't shed the first blood."

Hugglett spoon

Slobbers held on for his life and below him, he could see Geraintus struggling to save Yo-Yo on the front lawn. Gertrude was frozen to the top of the tree as if she'd been struck by lightning and Molly kept on chanting standing on the same branch to Slobbers' amazement.

Molly wailed the magical spell once more and sang the riddle again and Gertrude eventually squawked and fell to the lawn. Slobbers held on as he couldn't be seen to be sick or fall off. That wasn't going to happen; he just hoped the tree would stop shaking and Molly would finish.

Molly scattered a final round of angel dust from her tail and the tree spluttered, coughed, and stopped. This was so sudden, that Slobbers fell to the ground and landed on four feet as if he'd planned it and went straight to help Geraintus, as his thumb was stuck in between Yo-Yo's neck and collar.

Gertrude flew round the tree and Molly ran down seeing the problem with Yo-Yo.

"When did this start?" commanded Molly with one swish of her tail and a spell, *"Gembliani, milgi bach / Gembliani, meelgee bagh."*

The collar fell off Yo-Yo's neck and Geraintus' thumb was swollen. Slobbers started to roll around the lawn groaning, and he was sick.

"What's the matter Slobbers?"

"My tail is tingling; it's as if I'm getting a shock like those creatures gave me. I'm......."

"Goodness Geraintus, something's very wrong, he's fainted. I need to get them straight back to Ivor's. What's happening?" cried Molly trying not to panic.

"Gertrude, fly to the cave and get Harry the horse," as Gertrude flew away immediately. *"The Moonbeam can take you to the beach, where Harry can meet you. That will be quicker. I don't know what's going on Molly. The tree is spelled and is on our side. Gertrude or any of you can check the tree daily for any news. Once we've got our treasure returned, we can move the tree to its new home. We don't need to move it right now, it can wait. Quick, Gertrude is back. Let me help you get these two on the moonbeam."*

"Help me make a hammock with the overnight cloth, Slobbers packed for me," said Molly. *"Tie him inside and I'll be able to slide him over me. Yo-Yo curl up in a ball and sit inside my tummy flap. I shall fly us over; the Moonbeam is waiting,"* said Molly knowing this was really assessing her.

"Bring Yo-Yo's collar with you later, Geraintus. It's still hot to the touch, it needs to calm down."

Molly, with Slobbers on top of her and Yo -Yo underneath her, spelled herself by the Moonbeam to Pendine beach.

"Williannie grigolo, williannie grigolo," she repeated three times as she rose in the air. The beam tracking her, and a silver cloud enveloped them as she flew steadily murmuring her spell. They thudded and landed on Pendine beach. Yo-Yo rolled away from her, and Slobbers laid still, he was unconscious, and she had no way of carrying his weight even by spell.

She found Yo-Yo, who uncurled and looked at her quite feebly and curled back inside himself again and jumped on her neck for safety. She would have to wait for Harry, the horse; he should be on his way. She decided to pebble Garibaldi to inform him, where she was.

The pebble dispersed in front of her and as she focused down the beach, she could see something was coming towards her. She could make out Harry with his cart, but there was something else.

Gertrude flew towards her and flapped her wings,

"He's coming, he's coming," she squawked.

Harry the horse, turned into the strait of the beach and there were two dogs with him. They were all running fast, and Gertrude was flapping with excitement as Molly shouted at both Slobbers and Yo-Yo.

"It's Millie and Wibbly, look she's recovered come on," trying to revive them a little.

Wibbly helped her get both animals in the cart and she was pleased to see Millie was super fit and Wibbly was obviously jubilant too.

"Gertrude, lead the way," shouted Molly over her clucking as she stood on Harry's head as he galloped

down the beach. Millie and Wibbly Alf ran by their side as Molly keen to get back, knew there was another problem ahead. Let alone her two allies here needed a magical potion to make them better.

***

Ivor and Bedivere were nearly done with the clues. Garibaldi was beside himself, the pebble from Bethesda and Jethro was alarming and they couldn't wait for Molly to get back. Her summoning the horse and cart meant there had been a problem. A problem they didn't need as they had enough in the cave waiting to be solved. Garibaldi was thinking fast.

Things were going to get even trickier; he knew.

Chapter 13

Hopkin Paulinus.

Garibaldi placed the two platters of Welsh cakes on the table as the wizards shuffled all the papers, parchments, and puzzle to the end of the table. There was a lot to discuss with several pebbles still unopened from Ivor's requests regarding the riddle.

The door flung open as Millie and Wibbly ran in front of the party.

"Slobbers and Yo-Yo are hurt," Wibbly barked as Garibaldi flew outside with the wizards' robes flapping in the air as they followed.

The ginger twins with Molly were trying to carry Slobbers over the threshold and it was apparent that he was sick.

"Take them both in please," said Molly as Yo-Yo slid from her neck. Millie gently picked him up in her mouth and went inside.

"Good to see Millie has recovered, good job Wibbly."

"Yes, they've bonded," said Garibaldi not wishing to elaborate at that moment.

"Both their collars have been tingling as if they're trying to say something," said Bedivere as they all walked inside. The cats and Harry went back to

position as Gertrude flew to the shed to tell them what had happened.

Tudor, who was concerned by the lack of urgency around the place, started to look impatient.

"I know you've just walked in Molly but we've several things to be getting on with. I suggest we call Bethesda and Jethro over right away while Garibaldi and Bedivere are attending to Slobbers and Yo-Yo."

"I'm aware what's happened Tudor. Let the Wizards place their soothing potions on Slobbers and Yo-Yo first. They don't need to be invited to explain themselves, this very second," said Molly quite worried about her two friends.

*"I know it said, **"Friend not Foe,"** but something isn't right,"* said Garibaldi. *"Since you left Molly, we've had Millie's collar and Wibbly's both tingling to each other. We now have two extremely sick animals after you've spelled the tree, what's going on?*

"Whatever's happening, we need to act fast. I couldn't even spell Kester over this morning. My spells are weakening too."

"Tudor's right and I know you've got more pebbles to sift through, to see if there are castles with wishing wells, Bedivere. But we need some answers or new clues. Summon Bethesda and Jethro. They've defected from the Croggs, something's amiss there and we need to find out before we start again," said Molly knowing that Garibaldi had information to share. One thing at a time.

"We need to hide Millie as we need to be sure, they didn't have anything to do with her potential kill."

"Yes, Molly's right," said Ivor as he sent a pebble that moment to summon the two defectors to the cave.

The hovel screeched once again as Garibaldi went to check it, with Molly by his side. This gave them the chance to establish where the mass of dots were heading and where the three new dots were. Very soon, Molly would go and investigate.

"Cluck, cluck, cluck."

"We don't need anyone but Gertrude," smiled Molly at Garibaldi as they were deep in conversation in the parlour. *"I bet that's Bethesda and Jethro on their way already. Let's get ready for them; we need to remove everything from the table, just in case."*

Tudor and Ivor had already taken away all evidence of the puzzle, riddle and Millie had been hidden. Everyone was in their position awaiting the potential enemy to their door.

***

Further down the beach and walking with less confidence than they formerly felt were two defectors of the Croggs, Bethesda and Jethro. Jethro was so nervous his black eye kept turning round slowly making him look even more sinister than he did on occasions.

"Bethesda, what's in that basket you've brought as its glowing now and again making me feel even more

nervous," said Jethro his eye giving him away to how he felt.

Jethro was quite daunted by this plan of his brother. Having said that they'd be toast if they didn't join the enemy, the Croggs would have their heads. They didn't have many choices. He hoped it wasn't from the fat to the frying pan, as their old mum used to say.

The basket was glowing vividly as Jethro made comment and Bethesda quietly wished he had left the basket behind, on seeing the sight for himself.

"It's all of Millie's things, her blankets, her collars, and a standard, which to me looks like a Llewellyn standard, which is why the peace offering Jethro. We need to be on the right side of this battle. I don't trust the Croggs or even like what they're doing anymore. At least Ivor Llewellyn has a history of being fair."

"He might be fair, but he's weak Bethesda."

"But Molly's here Jethro, that's why, to give them their edge back. Less said the better, we're here."

They had walked towards the path, which had been lit for them, not noticing the cats, Gertrude, who was flying silently ahead. Harry pretended to look asleep as they walked up the path, the garden shed slightly ajar as Millie hid with Wibbly.

As they walked past them, Wibbly's link chain and Millie's own collar started to twinkle as if in response to the basket. Garibaldi had opened the door before they reached the step as he ushered them in towards the dining room, to meet the wizards.

"Thank you for seeing us," gushed Bethesda a bit daunted seeing everyone including Tudor, who looked infuriated with them.

"We've returned Millie's things and would like a chance to explain ourselves," said Jethro, his eye continuing to roll around taking in the contents of the room.

"Sit please," instructed Molly as they all nodded at the two nervous wizards as they sat. Garibaldi brought in some tea and Molly waited until they were ready.

"Are they alright?" asked Bethesda as he noticed a large cat and a tiny dog, curled up on the hearth in front of the fire.

"Yes, they were attacked earlier, but they'll be okay," said Ivor not wanting them to have any information.

"Millie was killed in an attack at Caernarvon, I think. We've come to bring her things to you and a chance to ask if we can defect from the Croggs to be at your side. We're not happy with Kentav Crogg and his army. He got Millie killed. I'm sorry," explained Bethesda placing the basket on the table for Garibaldi to rummage through.

"The thing is," Jethro added, *"The Croggs were sensible when we did the original battle, even when we lost. Something has happened to Kentav, and he's changed. He's determined to kill you all and gain the status of the First Family of Wales. We don't believe the treasure belongs to the Croggs, that's why we've left them. Killing Millie, as they thought she was a spy from*

here, was inexcusable. We haven't been happy since that incident."

The riddle flashed through the minds of the wizards, as they started to fidget uneasily as the men continued,

"We don't intend to return to St. Clears. We have a sister in Manorbier and we're going to live with her until we can set up our own casket and ministry business," explained Bethesda placing all their intents on the table.

"My bat saw you rummaging through my papers when you visited. What was all that about?" asked Tudor, who couldn't contain himself any longer.

"I was on orders from Kentav to find anything incriminating or a clue to where the spoon is hidden. I didn't look long or hard. I was already worried what had happened to Millie and something didn't feel right. I apologise for doing that."

"It's fine Bethesda, we don't have papers in our castles," said Tudor wanting them both to have false information, just in case.

"This basket is full of Llewellyn belongings. Millie is a Llewellyn dog," stated Garibaldi as he displayed the flag for all to see, the candle on the standard demonstrated it was a Llewellyn flag indeed.

"Oh, my goodness, I knew it," said Bethesda as he placed his hands over his face, in despair.

Before Molly could explain the door opened and Millie with Wibbly trying to prevent her, came bounding in excited. Her collar was talking to the collar in the basket and Wibbly's chain was also making a hissing noise.

"Why Millie, you're alive, thank goodness," cried Bethesda as he went towards her, and they embraced.

Tudor visibly relaxed as did Ivor. The way Bethesda and Jethro made a fuss of Millie had won them over instantly.

"Why do you want to defect?" asked Garibaldi being the cautious one, sliding the turquoise collar over Millie's head replacing the one she'd been found with to examine it properly.

"When Kentav came to the last meeting, his euphoria was so evident, he was bursting with confidence. He couldn't stop himself from telling everyone how easy stealing the coracle had been. He had his bug dog plan his next stage of the mission. He's unstoppable right now," said Jethro not noticing the wizards, especially Ivor cringing with the comment, of how easy it had been to steal the coracle.

"What are their plans?" asked Molly equally uneasy.

"The bug dogs, who attempted to kill Millie, are being programmed currently to kill and they are increasing their antenna capacity. This means with one turn their sparks will cause mayhem once they hit us or any building."

Bethesda continued,

"I was uncomfortable with Kentav, the way he is determined to kill you all; I couldn't stand it any longer. They don't have the right crest on their standard; we all know the treasure is rightfully yours."

"I think Kentav does too," said Ivor, *"But something else is driving him to make this hatred spill into a new battle. Where's he taking the coracle?"*

The hovel hissed quite loud once more as Tudor and Bedivere rushed to the parlour to check as Gari and Ivor, with Molly, continued to interrogate Bethesda and Jethro. Tudor and Elijas observed as they needed information to convince them even further, that they were on their side.

"The Croggs are on their way to Manorbier Castle with the coracle, that's what we've heard on the grapevine before we came here," said Bethesda.

"What else do you know?" asked Ivor pondering on this bit of news.

"Nothing much, but they were taking the Beggly army part of the way. Kentav wouldn't tell anyone where he's going to hide the coracle," added Jethro as he continued,

"I also heard him say that he was worried as the coracle was agitated and the moons inside the seat were flashing a silvery purple light, which didn't make sense to us."

"We're not sure, but they're on their way to Aberaeron ice cream factory to collect another thousand Begglys. He hasn't told anyone where they're heading from there. We overheard Manorbier, but we're not certain of anything else," said Bethesda wishing he'd more to give them.

"What about the spoon?" asked Molly as everyone held their breath.

"The Croggs haven't got it, and they presume you have. Once they've hidden the coracle, they're coming for you and the spoon, Molly."

Ivor paled at this information and looked at Garibaldi. Before anyone could say anything, Tudor and Bedivere returned convinced that the dots moving from Tregaron were the family with the chest and the spoon. Before they could discuss this, the basket slid off the table, turned itself upside down and spilled the contents over the floor.

Suddenly Wibbly Alf started to howl; Millie went outside and did the same. Garibaldi ran outside to check, their collars were dazzling all the animals, the collars were talking to each other. They both came into the cave and stood next to the heap of Millie's' belongings.

Yo-Yo uncurled himself as did Slobbers, both got up, shook themselves and went to the dogs, dazed but better. Molly joined them and immediately all the dogs and Slobbers were together, Garibaldi waved his hand in the air and spelled them.

"Why did you do that?" asked Elijas completely in awe of the wizards around him, the two newcomers and now Garibaldi.

"Good Gari. Call him, we need to know if the riddle means purple and turquoise collars," said Ivor. *"We also have an issue with the red one we buried, we need some answers,"* as Bethesda and Jethro looked scared.

Tudor got up as the hovel hissed loudly.

"I'll go and get hold of him now Ivor, before Gari's spell wears off."

Garibaldi stood still facing the frozen dogs and chanted aloud,

"Hopkin Paulinus come and see. Castles, friend, or treasure chest. It's you, or the whispering fig tree. Do we move north, south, or west? Molly, Millie, close your eyes, Wibbly Alf sits and watches deep. The collars won't tell lies; The answer is here; let's sleep."

"What does this mean?" whispered Jethro to Bethesda.

"Garibaldi has summoned the highest wizard in the land, which is why the hovel was screeching, but Tudor's checking it just in case.

Ivor got up.

"He's here."

Hopkin Paulinus stood on the porch as he bent his seven-foot frame and came in. His pointed hat made him even taller as he acknowledged everyone in the room. He swept his double cuffed cloak round the room, sending a flurry of silver moons over everyone, which jumped back onto the cuffs once he stood still.

"What do we have here, Ivor?"

"This is Bethesda and Jethro; they're defecting from the Croggs Hopkin."

Hopkin acknowledged a frightened looking Bethesda and Jethro and turned to the bunch of frozen animals on the carpet.

"Unfreeze them Gari, I want to meet the Magical Molly and her companions and look at these collars that are causing us some confusion."

"Datrys as unwaith, /Dahtreece are eenwaheeth," commanded Garibaldi.

Elijas immediately paid attention as how did this wizard know what was going on in Ivor' cave?

Molly, Millie and Wibbly Alf woke up and stared right into the wizard's face. Slobbers dropped his tail, and Yo-Yo immediately went under his belly for protection.

"It's ok everyone, I'm the eldest family wizard, Ivor calls me when we're in a pickle. Pleased to meet you all," as Hopkin bent to shake all the paws, noticing how powerful they all were, even Slobbers.

"Since Millie has arrived you've had a collar problem, I take it Ivor."

"*Yes Hopkin. Wibbly Alf has a link chain round his neck too, that's causing us confusion as he found it on his travels, looking for the spoon.*"

"*Let's have a look at the collars. Molly, are you wearing a purple one or the red one?*"

Surprised Hopkin new about the red collar, she immediately explained what had happened to it.

"*The red collar's important, let's keep it buried until we need it,*" said Hopkin as Molly looked at him in surprise.

"*Your purple collar is talking to Millie's' turquoise one, and the one she's wearing originally has a missing turquoise stone, which makes her a Llewellyn dog. This link chain, my.... my, you've found it......*" muttered Hopkin suddenly speechless for a second.

"*What is it Hopkin?*" asked his brother Ivor with Tudor sensing something too.

"*This link chain, Wibbly is wearing is more important than anything else you've right now,*" said Hopkin. "*Molly this chain links the Hugglett spoon to the Golden Coracle. Together they will make us all invincible and all your spells will return ten- fold. No - one is aware that this link chain is the key to the three treasures. Well done Wibbly for wearing it round your neck as no one will think its value, that way.*"

The collars continued to sparkle and twinkle to each other as Hopkin continued,

"*The Hugglett spoon's high in colour. The best part of it is purple with turquoise being the secondary colour. If there are any stones missing from collars, they will be turquoise ones. The spoon has a ten set turquoise stone which changes to purple in the moonbeam cycle of our calendar.*

It can detect us via our own moonbeam aura, up to thirty miles away. It's trying to contact you and because there are three chains here technically, the link chain and two collars, it's affecting them all. The spoon has a silvery purple and blue pouch if it's still with it. If it's come out of this pouch, it's certainly trying to contact us. It's exciting we may be closer than we think."

"*Why have Slobbers and Yo-Yo nearly been strangled when we've tried to link each other to the tree?*" asked Molly still worried about her colleagues.

"*Right, every time we go on a mission and we're not sure who's a Llewellyn; we must spell them our safety charm, to keep them from harm. Ivor or Garibaldi can give you instructions on the safety charm right away.*"

"*Don't waste any time, you must all go in convoy as often as you can. The more of you, the stronger the signal you're giving. The Hugglett spoon will start acting as a beacon and will take you to it,*" advised Hopkin sensing they weren't far away from capturing the spoon.

"*What about the riddle Hopkin? Do we decipher it and locate the spoon and coracle that way, can you advise us?*" asked Molly wishing to get on and retrieve these treasures as fast as possible.

"You have Manorbier on your radar from Bethesda's comments earlier. You need to find this spoon as quickly as possible and get on with your riddle, I can feel you're close. The rightful treasure chest we need will appear, I'm sure. Don't forget the treasure chest with the spoon isn't required, but then you've digested the riddle already, I can see," smiled Hopkin as he scanned the table full of papers. *"I must dash, have a meeting in Llandovery. Stay connected with me Molly,"* as he swished his triple pink cuffs of his cloak and muttered something as his cloak smothered everyone and the room filled with pink smoke. Hopkin Paulinus disappeared as promptly as he'd arrived.

The dogs and wizards spluttered everywhere as Gari went to open the front door, to let some air in. Bethesda and Jethro sat quite astounded by events and waited to see if they may be accepted by this eccentric and weird but friendly family.

"We need to move fast," said Molly gathering energy from Hopkin immediately. *"I think I'm going to investigate the three dots moving from Tregaron tonight. It's time to embrace you in our family, Bethesda, and Jethro. You can go and spy at Manorbier castle for us. If we think they're going there, then we must make sure the Coracle is seen being hidden there before we act. We can quickly retrieve the coracle, it's the spoon we urgently need."*

"Especially as the link chain, is crucial to attach them to the coracle, I didn't know that did you Ivor?"

asked Tudor amazed by their detached brother who never told them anything.

"*I certainly didn't know,*" said Ivor feeling a bit miffed but put it down to the uprising and battles going on with his long distant cousin Owain Glyndwr and the English.

"*Right, Bethesda, Jethro, come with me. I need to initiate you with our pebble system and give you double pins, as we will track you on our hovel,*" said Garibaldi moving them away from the table.

"*I'll go with you tonight,*" said Slobbers as Yo-Yo shook his little tail too.

"*No, neither of you are fit. As Hopkin mentioned the collars, I'll take Wibbly and Millie. The three collars along with our mooned capes should help us locate the spoon. If it's there as Hopkin suggests, we'll go once Bethesda and Jethro have gone to Manorbier. We need to get the map back on the table and the riddle answered Bedivere, Geraintus, and Elijas. Time is now of the essence,*" said Molly.

"*What if it's a trap?*" said Ivor getting worried.

"*For goodness' sake Ivor, let the magical dog do her stuff,*" said Tudor knowing he wasn't even strong enough to spell himself back to Caernarvon castle but didn't have the guts to tell anyone.

Bethesda and Jethro came back with Garibaldi feeling important. "*Let us know via pebble when you've found a hiding place and we'll instruct you from there,*" said Gari as everyone got up to see them off.

"Thank you," said Molly as she swished her tail and sprinkled angel dust over them as they departed feeling a part of the family.

"They'd better not defect from us," whispered Ivor as they closed the door behind them.

"It's ok Ivor, I've got it under control," said Gari smiling at Molly who nodded.

The hovel hissed again as Gari, Ivor and Molly ran to the parlour leaving Tudor, Bedivere and Elijas to complete the task of opening the pebbles from Ivor's' earlier request. Geraintus started making notes; his notebook was beginning to get muddled.

***

In the meantime, Hopkin Paulinus hovered in his glass pink coach down the beach, waiting for Molly and her two companions to investigate the moving party. She knew already that he was waiting for them, as they'd passed the information to each other as he'd left.

***

Molly, Wibbly Alf and Millie were ready to leave. It was apparent the family were in Narberth, resting for the night. It was time to find the lost treasure. They scampered down the path towards Hopkin Paulinus' glass coach. Slobbers and Yo-Yo were a bit put out but realised they were not fit for the new mission.

Gertrude clucked with excitement and flew inside the coach, without being asked. She wanted to be involved as she was instrumental in the communication system via the tree. She stopped clucking the minute she got close to Hopkin. That was a miracle. All they needed was a safe and swift flight to the area where the family were resting. The glass coach swirled into the air leaving a trail of pink smoke lingering over Saundersfoot beach.

Chapter 14

The Croggs and the Golden Coracle.

Kentav was having a bit of bother.

The Croggs and their supporters had been partying in Aberaeron, celebrating the capture of the Coracle. It was time to send everyone home including the Beggly army. Kentav didn't want them to know where he intended to hide his newfound treasure. However, his brothers, Ali and Trent were confused along with Zupp, head of the Beggly tribe, who'd been seconded to protect them.

"Kentav, we need at least the three main Begglys with us, for goodness' sake. We're about to walk into battle territory. Not only is Owain Glyndwr and his men battling with the English, but we've also local fighting going on; there's total unrest in the area. Surely, we need some help, as we'd be utterly useless without them," sighed Ali wondering whatever was wrong with his brother. He was losing the plot.

"Why do we need two coracles Kentav, I would also like to add?" asked Trent suspicious of his brother suddenly.

They'd stopped at Newcastle Emlyn, which meant he didn't want any of his hangers-on, supporters, and the main army to know where he was headed. In fact, he wasn't going to tell his brothers either until he was forced. It was crucial to keep the location a secret. Currently, they only knew part of his plan.

"Why can't they come to Manorbier with us, just to make sure we don't meet the Llewellyn's? I'm really surprised we haven't encountered them yet, Kentav. They might be waiting to ambush us, at Manorbier, we need to decide and prepare ourselves," said Trent not wishing to meet the Llewellyn army at all. He had scary memories of Ivor Ap Llewellyn's magical powers, they frightened him.

"He does have a point Kentav," agreed Ali sensing something wasn't quite right too.

"We need the second coracle for our provisions, and we've a decoy if we get ambushed," said Kentav knowing this made sense. He was right as both brothers nodded their heads in agreement.

"We ought to take the three top Begglys Kentav, at least they can protect us, and the others can go back to St. Clears and wait for our return."

"Yes Trent, you're right," said Kentav knowing this was his plan all along, but it was better coming from his brother, he knew they didn't trust him.

"These Begglys can wait for us outside the gates while we get Katrin to help us hide the coracle. Otherwise,

it may get messy," outlined Trent knowing he was also right.

He was so pleased that Kentav had decided to hide the coracle at his girlfriend's castle; he was beside himself with pride. It was also a surprise as Katrin Crogg was half Llewellyn but suddenly this didn't upset Kentav. Fraternising with the enemy had led to their fourths' brothers' demise. His burnt out hutlet at the bottom of the hill was a constant reminder how much hatred was felt for the Llewellyn's.

"I'm more concerned that we haven't seen the Llewellyn's yet. We need to move along as I don't want to meet them either," said Ali deciding there and then that this was his last mission. He was going to leave for distant lands the minute they returned; he'd had enough of these silly battles and fights. And to what end?

"Leave the three main Begglys here, Ali's right, we need to move along," instructed Kentav as he moved away pulling one coracle. Trent pulled the second one as Ali gave everyone instructions to go home.

Kentav had an excellent plan which he hadn't unravelled yet. He wasn't going to leave the coracle under the very nose of the Llewellyn's, no chance, he had a better idea. In the meantime, they all continued in single file through the fields as the three Begglys zapped in front behind and around them, checking for anyone ahead and in several fields away, to be sure. His plan was fool proof, and he decided not to tell them. He didn't believe his brothers had the same loyalty as he.

He was the eldest and had a reason he felt different from the others. Someone had to take charge of the community, and he was the greatest leader and head of the family. He'd wait until they were nearer and then he'd put his plan in place. They would soon realise why he had two coracles.

Zupp, Zap and Zipp just buzzed around them and continued to watch. They were silent, but their antennae moved around constantly making anyone dizzy if they were watching. They were relentless and their oval pearlescent bodies glimmered in the early evening dusk, making them hard to spot. This of course was a good thing.

"We'll camp here for the night," suggested Kentav, which was a strategic place to stop. They were going to Llawhaden and not Manorbier in the morning, but no one knew yet.

While Ali and Trent were sorting out provisions, Ali's comment started to bother Kentav as he sat in the middle of the two coracles. The Begglys continued to check the fields adjoining them for enemies or unwanted threats. It was strange; Ivor Llewellyn hadn't marched to St. Clears with his wizards and troops demanding the coracle returned. The family had indeed gone quiet.

This started to bother Kentav a bit more than he realised. Ali was right, this wasn't usual. What that really meant Kentav wasn't quite sure, as his train of thought was interrupted by Ali and Trent bringing their supper over to join him.

They ate in silence and Kentav prepared his pipe, he wasn't sure when to bring up the subject of the change of venue. He didn't want a fuss. As if on cue the coracle started to swivel and glow in the darkness.

"Oh, my goodness Trent put the blankets and coats over it, look it's glowing and. ....How are we going to stop it drawing attention to us?" panicked Kentav.

"Calm down Kentav, it's only a coracle," said Trent as he shoved all their belongings over it, to try and stop it from glowing.

"Who's going to see it in the dark Kentav? Just keep calm, it'll be all right," said Ali trying to sound convinced but wasn't entirely sure himself what to make of it.

"It's certainly agitated," said Trent as he filled it completely with all the belongings from the second coracle.

"The Begglys will soon tell us if there's anyone about Kentav. Stop shouting, you're not helping it. It's noticing your stress levels. I don't know," said Ali now a bit worried.

"I suggest we sit in the coracle next to it and hold it down and try and rest. The Begglys are patrolling around us, we can't do anything else," said Trent as Ali agreed and Kentav sighed, and he knew that he needed to tell them both in the morning he'd changed the plan.

***

A few miles East of where the Croggs had set up camp, a horse and cart entered a field for shelter. The young family decided to stop for the night and continue their journey in the morning. The young boy was tired, and the mother wrapped him in blankets as they huddled together under the cart to keep warm. The treasure chest sat on the cart, untouched with the lid closed.

The boy was holding something as he slept; it was a spoon, very unusual in style and colourful. His mother noticed and as she took it quietly away from her boy, it glowed and shone a bright light in her face. She smiled and placed it back in the silk pouch that lay beside it. Her son had found it in the chest as she put it back inside for safe keeping.

***

Overhead, and at the same time, a flock of wild birds flew on a mission instigated by Robin and Rudge. They observed as they flew over the horse and its party, the glowing of an object being placed inside a treasure chest, and they knew immediately. As they flew further, they saw the Golden Coracle suffocating under a pile of blankets and provisions, the glow of its aura agitated. They returned to base command; they had lots to tell Robin.

***

Morning arrived, it was drizzly with low cloud, and Kentav was debating how to change the route to hide his coracle. Before he could broach the subject, Beggly one Zupp, came whizzing up to Trent very animated, his antennae spinning round making Trent feel quite queasy. He felt even more worried and sick when he received the unwelcome news which he had to relate to Kentav and Ali.

"What is it?" said Ali, sensing trouble.

"Owain Glyndwr is in the area Kentav. His army is on route this way. If he sees us, he'll hang us as it's obvious we've stolen the coracle."

This was indeed music to Kentav's ears as he pretended to look aghast and troubled.

"We need to detour immediately," he said trying not to sound jubilant.

"What do you have in mind?" asked Ali surprised.

"I've got a friend in Llawhaden Castle; it's only a few miles west of here. I suggest we move quickly there to avoid Owain. If we leave right away, the mist may help us stay unnoticed. Quick Ali, get the Begglys to go west and start checking for oncoming armies or Llewellyn's even," instructed Kentav sounding more relieved than authoritative, he was only glad his plan had worked with no effort from him.

Ali was suddenly very suspicious and knew that Kentav wasn't being truthful with them. He decided he would keep a close eye on his brother and see what transpired from this next event.

"What about Katrin at Manorbier?" asked Trent knowing she was risking it as it was, hiding the coracle. They'd be arriving later than scheduled, what should he do?

"We'll lay low for a day at Llawhaden Trent and then we'll go to Manorbier. We can't afford to be seen by Owain's army. They'll have our heads for this. She'll just have to presume we're running late."

"I suppose you're right. There's not much I can do about it," said Trent knowing his Katrin will be anxious and worried about them being late.

"Come on, let's go," said Kentav as they quietly left the field and entered another one to avoid the route that Owain and his men were walking.

The sentry on duty on the outskirts of Llawhaden shocked Trent and Ali as they'd not anticipated there would be guards outside the gates. Kentav took this all in his stride and immediately sent Zupp with instructions to inform the cat, they'd arrived.

Trent looked at Ali and they both knew that this had been his plan all along, but both kept quiet. Separately they would be both glad to see the end of this mission, they'd both made different plans but none of them included Kentav.

The big cat sat on top of the turret looking down at the party to the side of the castle.

"What do we have here then," he thought as he swung his great big tail over the wall and observed. He noticed the oval creatures with antennas spinning and decided it was best not to kill them until he knew who they were. He sat and watched.

The sentry suddenly disappeared with a sound of a horn, and he watched three little people with three bugs quickly enter the castle grounds. His master, Thomas Beckett walked towards the party to greet them, this was indeed peculiar.

"Kentav, it's been too long. How are you?" asked Thomas Beckett and both Trent and Ali knew that Kentav had lost the plot. They were with Ivor Ap Llewellyn's old friend and suddenly he was friends with the Croggs?

"We're on our way to Manorbier and need to stay overnight Thomas. I hope this doesn't inconvenience you at all."

"Goodness no, indeed, you must all eat and tell me what you've all been doing these past few years. Come, come, inside," he waved his hand beaming at having guests for the night.

The big cat smelt a big rat and keeping track of three ugly black creatures decided to get closer to listen to what was going down.

Over dinner, it dawned on both Trent and Ali what Kentav was doing. In the middle of the night, Ali watched Kentav move the Golden Coracle to the dungeon. He observed him locking the gate of the basement. Ali was furious as he knew that Trent's girlfriend was expecting the real one. He was going to march to Manorbier with the decoy coracle. He must think that Trent and he were stupid. Ali decided to say nothing and wait to see if Kentav would tell them in the morning that he'd hidden the real coracle at Llawhaden Castle. He'd organised this from the beginning. The sooner Ali could get home and leave the better. He felt sick with the betrayal.

In the morning as they departed and thanked Thomas for his hospitality Kentav mentioned,

"We've left a coracle here Thomas. We'll collect it on our return if that's all right?"

"Yes of course, where have you put it?"

"It's in the dungeon, out of harm's way."

"No problem. Look forward to seeing you soon then."

The Begglys went in front, the sentry not in sight as the three brothers walked away with one coracle. The cat confused with his master's behaviour and even more intrigued with the coracle that was in their dungeon.

Kentav, feeling euphoric and important marched ahead pulling the coracle with Trent and Ali in stunned silence. Kentav was close to being head of the realm and close to owning all these castles. So close with one more treasure to find, as he knew it. He had no idea about the treasure chest, but right now he was feeling quite important.

Chapter 15

The Romani family.

Since Hopkin Paulinus had said, "*Follow the riddle*," Ivor and the wizards had started to focus intently on the unanswered pebbles. They recognised that their powers were dwindling. Tudor was agitated for this very reason and Garibaldi knew he needed to somehow keep their spirits up.

Gari's teapot full of his special brew with added substances would maintain their focus and high spirits. Geraintus, with his notebook and pen ready was already making notes from the responding pebbles.

"*Read the riddle Bedivere, Geraintus make notes and Elijas, start opening the responses, we must haste,*" instructed Ivor as he gulped the first mouthful of Gari's tea and immediately smiled, looked at Tudor and poured himself and Tudor some more.

***

Hopkin was pleased with his lesson. Molly, Wibbly and Millie had been responsive with their new spells and Gertrude hadn't clucked once during the journey. The magical coach was nearing Narberth, and they decided to hover close to a field where they believed the family were camping.

The slipper steps started to hang from the coach as it glided closer to land and Hopkin nodded as the glass doors opened and the dogs and a silent hen disappeared. Hopkin promised to stay connected, and Molly felt a bit more in control having had lessons and reassurance from the great Hopkin Paulinus.

"Cluck, cluck," squawked Gertrude as Wibbly immediately used his tail to acknowledge her to be quiet.

"Shh," whispered Millie the same time.

"Shh come on, we must move to the hedges in case we're seen. Gertrude be silent and fly overhead to see if you can find the family. Check the few fields either side of us," instructed Molly. *"It will give me time to spell Wibbly and Millie for protection cover."*

Molly gathered round the two dogs and muttered her new spell, learnt from Hopkin.

"Marddanhaden cochwyn, amharchus taith/ Mahrthan hahden coghween amhahrchees taheeth."

A puff of green smoke appeared, and she knew it had worked. The smoke subsided and Gertrude appeared from her surveillance and landed on Millie to report. Her lack of clucking was evident, as she'd learnt from Hopkin too.

"The horse and cart with the family are two fields away, which is the good news. The unwelcome news is that Owain Glyndwr and his warriors are three fields away and heading towards the area we need."

"How many warriors?" asked Wibbly.

"Thousands follow me."

"*Wait,*" instructed Molly. "*This is what we'll do, gather round.*"

They huddled together and once Molly had given her instructions, they left following Gertrude, who flew hedge height, enough for the dogs to see her, but not for anyone to notice a flying hen. Gertrude was excited and knew once she saw them into the field, she was to leave and fly to the whispering fig tree. There she would gather all the latest information or messages, relay hers and return to the Cave.

They entered the field and to their amazement the family were tucked up near the hedge, asleep covered in rugs, with their belongings covered with thick blankets on the cart. They were all huddled under the cart to keep warm and shelter from the weather. The horse was standing but sleeping. Even from the little distance they were from the family, Molly could see the treasure chest was under the blankets.

They all looked at each other and they started their plan. Molly waved her paw, and the horse and cart changed into two giant onions. The family under the cart went into a deeper sleep. A puff of green smoke appeared once again and Millie and Wibbly ran to the cart and moved the treasure chest away as Molly pulled away the blankets.

"Cluck, cluck," squawked Gertrude once again as Molly realised the army were heading towards their field.

"Hurry, check the chest Millie, quick."

Millie and Wibbly opened the chest, the lid heavier than they'd anticipated. A flash of piercing light struck them all as the lid opened. The collars on each dog started to tingle and made the dogs agitated. Trying to keep control, Molly shouted as she was keeping an eye on the family and the onions.

"Wibbly, Millie can you see the spoon?"

The light dazzled the two dogs as they rummaged through the chest. Suddenly a flash of light and a silver and purple silk pouch jumped out of the chest and flew towards Molly, who caught it in her paws.

Immediately the gates of the field opened, and Gertrude started to cluck as loud as she dared.

Millie was choking as her collar tightened and Molly was struggling to keep the spoon in its pouch.

"Let it go," said Wibbly his link chain strangling him as Gertrude flew round them in a panic. The onions changed to the horse and cart and the family were waking up as Owain and his three men ahead of the warriors walked towards them in utter surprise.

The spoon jumped from the pouch and attached itself to Wibbly's link chain and the collars of the dogs subsided and stopped tingling. Molly looked at the family, looked at Owain and stood motionless for a moment. The three dogs knew what was going to happen next and waited for Owain to say something.

The family cowered under the cart, near the hedge on seeing the army of men. The spoon needed to be covered for protection. It was also hefty and Wibbly was now unable to move. Mobilising them as originally planned wasn't going to work. Molly thought fast as Owain approached as he witnessed a bazaar scene as Gertrude was clucking overhead, more from fear and nerves than excitement.

"Millie, jump on the cart with the chest and Wibbly, quick."

"Molly, good heavens whatever are you doing here of all places?" said Owain as he stood there in full armour with three men around him sporting long spears.

"I can't explain now Owain. We need to leave. Ivor will explain by a pebble."

With all her might and newly learnt spells from Hopkin, Molly swished her tail and jumped on the cart. To Owain's amazement all the belongings dispersed from the cart to the ground, leaving the chest, as they watched her float away on the cart, unhinged from the sleeping horse.

Molly murmured the spell furiously as Gertrude clucked and flew ahead. A puff of pink cloud arrived, and the cart flew into it and disappeared as the dogs heard a squawk and a thud as Gertrude plummeted to her death.

Molly knew she had to concentrate on her spell and fly them to the cave. There was no time to rescue Gertrude; one of the warriors had naturally thought they were stealing the family's treasure as indeed they were. The lid was closed, and she knew her two dogs were inside with the spoon. It hadn't been that difficult a task. The spell she was using was linked to the cave. Sure, enough as the cart glided to a gentle thud on the beach, the ginger twins with Harry the horse arrived in seconds to hitch the cart and take them back to the cave.

"Beniali, beillioni/Beneealee, beylleone," whispered Molly as the chest lid opened and Wibbly and Millie were entwined inside. The spoon was squashed but safe amongst the two dogs and she closed the lid. Both dogs seemed spelled to the spoon, but they'd retrieved it; she wasn't going to lose it again.

"Has Gertrude gone to the whispering fig tree?" asked Ginger One who was sitting in the cart with Molly.

"She's gone," said Molly absent-mindedly for a second, she didn't want to take away the euphoria felt by the cats and Harry as they'd been so excited to meet them on the beach. Her plan had worked, she'd found the spoon but in turn they'd lost a family member. The poem had been right.

Molly hoped Yo-Yo and Slobbers were better. She needed these two dogs unleashed from the spoon and then as a family they needed to locate the Coracle immediately. Harry came to a halt outside the cave and

Garibaldi was at the front door. He came rushing out with Bedivere and they carried the chest indoors.

Slobbers was all over the chest as was Yo-Yo and there was a buzz of excitement in the cave as the wizards all chatted at once as Ivor opened the lid. Wibbly and Millie were indeed asleep, and Tudor muttered something as did Ivor and the dogs opened their eyes.

"Get them out of there," said Garibaldi as he rushed to the pantry to locate a magic potion.

Molly was feeling euphoric and sad at the same time. There was no time to waste as she watched the wizards disentangling the weak dogs and Ivor was attempting to remove the spoon from Wibbly's link chain.

"I'd forgotten how heavy this spoon is," said Ivor as Tudor helped him prise it away from Wibbly's neck. It jumped back inside its pouch and sprung towards Yo-Yo who was nearly knocked over by its weight.

"We need to spell it," said Molly, *"It's not safe, it keeps moving around."*

"If I recall it needs to be soothed with a turquoise collar and we need to keep it hidden," said Ivor thrilled at having the spoon back in his possession after all these years.

Molly sat at the table and the spoon was locked in the parlour for the evening. Silence fell over the dining room as suddenly everyone realised that Gertrude hadn't gone to the whispering fig tree, she'd been killed by a spear and left on the field for dead.

"We couldn't bring her home we had to leave, I'm so sorry," whispered Molly as everyone nodded and Garibaldi got up and went to make more tea.

"We need to get back to matters in hand," said Geraintus. *"I shall leave right away as the tree needs to be checked. We can bring the tree here at the proper time, as we may be missing vital intelligence from the bird kingdom if we don't check it daily. Elijas, here's my notes, I'll return in the morning with an update."*

"At least we haven't cast the first stone," said Elijas suddenly.

"What do you mean?" asked Molly.

"The riddle said, we mustn't kill first, Owain's men have killed Gertrude. We can march on knowing we haven't been the first to shed blood."

"Yes, we also need to dispose of the chest," said Garibaldi, *"That's another line of the riddle we've achieved tonight. Excellent job guys."*

Geraintus said farewell and the Wizards returned to the dining room table to complete the findings with Molly. Wibbly Alf and Millie were curled up on the hearth, a sleeping draft and soothing potion had taken effect, with Yo-Yo and Slobbers close by.

Molly looked on and realised they'd all been affected by the spoon or events leading to retrieving it. She could only hope that locating the Coracle was going to be as straightforward. However, something was telling her that this was not likely.

"*Let's see what castles have the answers for us, Elijas. The sooner we narrow it down, the sooner we can all find the Coracle,*" said Molly knowing that this was going to be the most challenging part of all.

Chapter 16

Magical Molly and wizards discover a clue.

The treasure chest was moved to the kitchen to be disposed of, at Garibaldi's discretion. All the windows were bolted, the fireplace was blocked, and the cave went into lock down. All the secret passages were sealed, and Tudor disappeared to secure the hovel and check any movements on it. The Hugglett spoon was a precious family heirloom and had been missing for so long, the risk to lose it currently felt like a heavy burden.

Whilst Ivor and Garibaldi were securing the cave, Molly and Bedivere, with Elijas' notes started to discuss the findings from the pebbles. The map covered the table, and the riddle had at least a few lines crossed through, making Molly feel they were finally getting somewhere.

The dogs and Slobbers were asleep on the hearth and the Hugglett spoon was amongst them, hidden by all the fur. Everyone seemed suddenly at peace. Molly, knowing the wizards were becoming powerless by the minute let her thoughts concentrate on the evidence the wizards had collected.

Rat, tat, tat.

Garibaldi rushed to the front door before anyone blinked and received a pebble from the goose. Ginger One was also there with a message for Garibaldi as he nodded and closed the door quickly.

"Who's it from?" asked Molly.

"Bethesda and Jethro are watching Manorbier castle and can confirm the Croggs are marching towards it. They're pulling a coracle."

"Thank goodness, we waited," said Molly.

Bedivere and Elijas had something to say but Molly waved her tail as Ivor and Tudor came back to their chairs.

"Who's coming Gari?"

"There are about fifty warriors marching towards us carrying Owain's standard and some are on horses," said Gari quietly trying not to panic. *"I've instructed the twins and Harry outside to stand in front of the main path until we're ready to greet them."*

"Whatever do they want?" said Ivor ruffled by this sudden sign of war.

"Call on Hopkin Molly," instructed Ivor as he went outside, as he was head of the family. *"Come and join me outside as soon as you've summoned him."*

Molly didn't need to be asked twice as she got up and went to the main hall, swished her tail, spun three times, and chanted the spell for Hopkin aloud,

"Caiooiac, Caiooiac/ Kah-eeoack, Kah-eeoack"

An enormous puff of pink cloud and smoke appeared in the hallway as the contingent of furry animals by the hearth, all woke up spluttering with the intensity of the intrusion. Hopkin appeared in the centre of the cloud, his double cuffed pink robes swirling around causing even more mayhem.

"Meri a Mari, Meri a Mari," instructed Garibaldi waving his hand three times to his left and the cloud disappeared leaving Hopkin grinning at everyone.

"For goodness' sake Hopkin, you need to use some discretion, the dogs are recovering from an attack from the spoon," said Tudor agitated with his older but not always wiser brother.

"I'll secure the cave and contents Molly. Go outside with Ivor to see what they want. It's you they'll want to speak with, I'm sure."

Molly smiled and went to join Ivor; Garibaldi followed which left Hopkin to be entertained by Tudor, Bedivere and Elijas.

The army of men were indeed marching deliberately towards the cave and even though Ivor looked confident, he was shaking in his boots. Molly could sense this, and she moved slightly ahead of him, she wasn't afraid.

As the head warrior approached, he stopped and in a crisp voice,

"Permission Ivor Ap Llewellyn to enter your premises."

"Granted," replied Ivor who sounded more authoritative than he felt.

The Ginger twins moved aside as did Harry the horse and disappeared.

"A message from Owain," said the soldier who cleared his throat and held up a parchment which the warrior read,

"I realised my error of weeks gone by as I saw Molly tonight with the treasure chest. I gave your treasure away innocently a few weeks ago. Forgive my actions and to compensate, I send you fifty men and some horses to assist you in your quest to marry the Coracle with the spoon. We serve and protect our lord and master. Succeed and we shall be over the moon."

Ivor nearly fainted as he gathered this was help arriving at a grand scale.

"Who's in command of the men, soldier?"

"I am. My name is Iswallt and at your service. This is for you too. We attacked your hen before Owain commanded us to cease fire. We didn't realise she was protecting you. We thought you'd want to bury her here," said the soldier as he turned to his man who gave him a casket, which he handed to Ivor.

"Thank you," said Molly suddenly speechless for a second. *"We will bury her at dawn."*

"Can you camp on the beach this evening, Iswallt? We will have instructions for you at dawn to assist us locate the Coracle and Spoon," said Molly, not wishing

for anyone to know they had possession of the Hugglett spoon.

"Slobbers or one of my aides will instruct you in the morning."

Iswallt nodded, retreated a few steps, bowed at Ivor Ap Llewellyn with respect and turned and made his way to his waiting men. They all proceeded to the beach as instructed.

Molly swished her tail, and all the animals followed Ivor and her into the cave. The casket was laid on the table and everyone fell silent for a moment. Hopkin was standing in the hallway having checked all the dogs for collar injuries and had declared everyone fit and healthy. The atmosphere in the cave was of mixed emotion and sadness.

"We must continue," said Hopkin. *"Gertrude was instrumental in assisting you this far. I have soothed the spoon and it's now hiding in the cushion on the couch, Yo-Yo has been assigned to watch over it. Wibbly Alf and Millie need to keep close to it too. I'd forgotten how sensitive it is. You must all remember any sudden calamities inside the cave, and it will take off on its own volition. It needs to be spelled daily to your collars,"* instructed Hopkin, as he bowed towards Ivor. He spun round and with one strike of his double cuffed cloak, disappeared through the sealed passageway causing an immense amount of pink cloud, yet again.

"I wish he wouldn't do that," spluttered Tudor as he waved his hand, and the windows all opened and quickly closed by the swish of Molly's tail.

"We can't afford to open the windows, Tudor. We all know the spoon could take off at any minute. The sooner we can link it to the coracle with Wibbly's chain the better."

The miners' lantern in the hallway started to spew out black smoke and the bulbous tips of the chandeliers above started to turn black, and the cave suddenly went cold.

"What's going on?" said Yo-Yo from the fireplace, frightened and moved closer to Slobbers' fat tummy.

Gari looked at Molly and Molly looked at Tudor. Suddenly the black curling smoke turned to a bottle green, and Molly knew. The second door to the secret passageway crashed open, even though it was sealed and Geraintus fell into the hall spluttering and surrounded by a green cloud, making his green-tinged skin look even more sinister.

His cumbersome frame moved quickly towards the dining room table, where the family were sat. He nodded at Molly a bit sheepish and glanced at the animals by the fireplace.

"What's happened Geraintus?" asked Ivor sensing this was not his normal behaviour.

"I've been taking messages from the whispering fig tree as you know. The most important message is from Robin and Rudge, our red kites."

"At last," said Tudor as he took a Welsh cake from the platter Gari was taking round the table.

"The thing is, they saw a day ago, the Crogg contingent and a few thousand of those bug dogs, walking towards Narberth pulling two coracles. The three brothers are together."

Bedivere went pale at hearing this and started to look at the map intently.

"Are you sure, it was two coracles?" asked Molly as both Ivor and Tudor got up to study the map.

"Yes, it was definitely two, why" asked Geraintus going greener than usual at being doubted.

"Bethesda and Jethro have sent us a pebble, confirming they've seen the Croggs at Manorbier with one coracle. We've no reason to doubt their ability to count or lie to us," said Tudor frowning and studying the map.

"When was this Geraintus?" asked Molly trying to ascertain the timing of this sighting.

"More or less the same time as you were retrieving the spoon."

"Yes, Gertrude did say the Croggs were on the same route as us, but we didn't stay to find out once we'd captured the spoon. We needed to get out of the field and of course Owain's men didn't help matters."

"They were seen going west from Narbeth; Robin did say that they saw the men in the field and a horse

and cart. It must have been the same time as you were there."

"So, what's happened to one coracle between Narberth and Manorbier?" asked Bedivere as he started to look at the map for both locations.

"Bethesda and Jethro have definitely confirmed that the Croggs are within distance of Manorbier Castle," said Geraintus.

"Gari, send them another pebble, with instructions we must know precisely what's happened to the Croggs and this one coracle," said Molly getting excited.

She swished her tail round the room scattering angel dust and the dogs on the hearth started to come out of their slumber. The spoon began to fidget inside the cushion and Yo-Yo jumped on the sofa, retrieved it, and dragged it to the middle of the dogs for safety.

"We need a list of all castles and potential hiding places for a coracle, right away. We've got fifty men outside which we can split in half, and they can do the legwork for us. We can find this coracle very quickly."

Chapter 17

The Golden Coracle's whereabouts.

The excitement within the cave started to build, they knew this was the missing coracle; the news brought by Geraintus was significant. Garibaldi went to make more tea and Geraintus departed by the second passageway. It was imperative he return to collect more information.

"We must relocate this tree once we know what we're doing," said Molly.

"Yes, you're right. Those birds have come up trumps already. Let's get to this map and riddle, as those men need some instructions from you at dawn," suggested Elijas feeling a bit braver than normal because Geraintus had left him his notes.

Rat tat tat.

"Gari, be quick, we need to get on with this," said Ivor going through the pebbles as he looked quite frail suddenly.

"It's Bethesda and Jethro. They've confirmed its one coracle and the Croggs are close to the castle. No other news yet."

"Right Wibbly, Millie, can you get outside with Slobbers. We need full patrols, even though we have warriors on the beach. One coracle could mean the brothers have split up; we don't want unnecessary visitors tonight. Yo-Yo, the spoon will start getting agitated when we start talking about castle locations. I want you to alert us if it goes crazy when we say a castle place or name."

Slobbers was Top Cat, and he was with the Top Dogs. He couldn't ask for anything else. He knew his collar had been tingling with the others, he wasn't sure what this meant, but he didn't mind not looking after the spoon. He was more than happy to be organising the security outside with the Ginger twins and Wibbly Alf. Slobbers also realised that Molly knew his history and he didn't have to prove himself to be part of this family.

Millie was also happy to be amongst the Llewellyn's. She couldn't believe her luck. She'd thought during that attack that she wouldn't survive, let alone find herself where she belonged and fully recovered. She was also delighted to have found Wibbly, who adored her.

Yo-Yo, in turn, was feeling a bit daunted by this sudden surge in responsibility. However, he knew he was a powerful tiny dog, and this was why he'd been sent with Molly, to assist her find the spoon.

The wizards were methodically going through the pebbles, checking against the list Geraintus had written.

Elijas started to read the riddle and Molly realised that the Croggs had given them their best clue yet.

"Elijas read the riddle out loud, let's comment per line everyone and get to the castles we need to search," instructed Molly.

"First line, "Death is imminent for a friend, not foe." "

"Gertrude is dead, we can cross a line through it," said Bedivere.

"No," said Tudor, *"Owain's lot are protecting the beach with fifty of his men right now, as a condolence for killing a friend, not a foe. I don't think we should ignore this line at all. We need to be mindful, we're not out of the woods yet, and a confrontation is inevitable."*

"I think Tudor's right, let's get to the next line Elijas," said Ivor agreeing. Quietly he hoped there wouldn't be any bloodshed; he didn't think he could withstand any conflict.

"Do we all agree with Ivor?" asked Gari round the table.

Everyone nodded and Molly waved her tail as Elijas continued,

"I'll miss the next line as it's about magic, the next line says,

""Eagles are coming; red kites, or bats, no""

"I have a bat," said Tudor feebly trying to solve the poem himself.

"Robin and Rudge are protected red kites. Although they're sending us messages, they'll not lead us to the coracle, not directly anyway," said Ivor.

"Does anyone on the castle list have eagles," enquired Molly looking at Elijas for his list.

Elijas scanned the list of responses from the pebbles as Ivor started to fidget uncomfortably in his chair and Gari suddenly clicked, his astonishing memory went into overdrive, and he couldn't stop himself.

"Tell them Ivor for goodness' sake."

"Ivor, what is it," asked Molly.

"Castell Coch has a history of Golden Eagles; they must have gone now, but they were there to protect a treasure chest, which looks similar to the one in the hallway," he sighed.

"Ivor, pull yourself together," snapped Tudor.

"Elijas look for their response on your list. Ivor tell us the story it could be important," said Molly who realised that Ivor wasn't as forthcoming as he should be.

"Quite a few years ago, our second cousin, Gilbert De Clare handed the keys to Ifor ap Meurig, our first cousin. He declared this was one of our castles and only a Llewellyn could live in it, along with the coveted treasures. To secure the treasure on site, he transformed two of his finest warriors into Golden Eagles to look after his castle and protect his wealth within the chest. The

Golden Eagles were to keep everyone apart from the Llewellyn family from entering the castle gates."

"*Are those eagles there now?*" asked Molly, looking at Elijas.

Bedivere answered instead,

"*Yes, when we sent a pebble to every castle, the goose returned it unopened. When we asked him why, he stated he was attacked by two irate Golden Eagles. I apologise I didn't think until now, but this is significant.*"

"*Castell Coch is rightfully ours, but I've neglected the need to go and live there.*"

"*We all want to live in the rightful castle, this is high on the list,*" said Molly as she nodded for Elijas to start a new list. "*We can worry about the eagles when we're able to take the coracle and spoon there. The chest is obviously there, that saves us looking for another one.*"

"*Right, Elijas everyone. Castell Coch has a treasure chest protected by two Golden Eagles, this is part of the treasure we're looking for,*" said Molly now pacing round the table. "*Next line, Elijas.*"

Before Elijas could continue the miners,' lantern went white and frothy and everyone waited for the goose to knock, which was within seconds and Garibaldi retrieved the pebble.

"*It's Bethesda. Croggs are hiding in the church grounds with one coracle, await instructions.*"

"*We'll send half of the warriors to Manorbier to investigate, send a pebble to them Gari. Warn them that thirty soldiers will be marching over to inspect the castle, and they belong to us, but let's continue as we need to send the others somewhere else."*

Gari rushed outside and gave Slobbers instructions as he sat on the mat outside.

"Next line is..., **"find the clue an ancient place with a wishing well.""**

"*All the castles are ancient,*" said Gari as he closed the front door.

"*How many near Narbeth have wishing wells?*" asked Molly.

"*None that we know about,*" said Bedivere.

"*I think we should concentrate on all the castles in the region of Narbeth and not worry about wishing wells,*" said Tudor.

Everyone agreed.

"*We have six to consider then,*" said Bedivere with his wand pointing out the castles on the map as Elijas read them out.

"*We've got Pembroke, Manorbier, Carew, Llawhaden, Llansteffan and Laugharne. The rest are too far away from the Croggs supposed route.*"

"*Laugharne and Llansteffan are both out,*" said Ivor, "*My half-brothers live there, and their pebbles confirm there's nothing amiss in either castle or have wished us luck in finding the treasure.*"

"*That leaves four,*" said Gari.

"Manorbier is obvious; where else do we need to go?"

"We should pay the remaining four a visit; we can't afford to miss anything. Once the Croggs hide or destroy that coracle, they'll be marching here for a confrontation about the spoon. We need to make decisions tonight."

"Let's continue with the riddle Elijas," said Molly.

"Next line, **"Purple is strong, but there is turquoise blue. Not to paddle but to carry Coracle Gold. Nesta, Helen of Wales, says it's true."**

"We need to investigate Carew Castle. Helen, Nesta has a clue for us," said Molly.

"I don't think she'll have the clues we need," said Tudor.

"Shall we send the second lot of troops there to investigate then?"

"Why don't we go to Carew and send the troops to Pembroke or Llawhaden?" said Gari.

Elijas paled and shouted,

"This is strange, everyone. I didn't notice until now. Out of these four castles, Thomas Beckett at Llawhaden never responded to the pebble."

"Why would that be?" asked Bedivere as he looked straight at Ivor who flinched.

"I'm in a middle of a disagreement with him, that's why," said Ivor getting agitated as Tudor sighed. Molly looked at Garibaldi who went red in the face as she realised suddenly that Ivor wasn't helping at all about family matters. This wasn't being loyal to their quest.

"Maybe he ignored the pebble as we're not talking."

"I think this is significant," said Molly. *"It's easily on route for the Croggs; Thomas Beckett could be swayed to be disloyal if he's fallen out with you. It would be easy to hide one coracle there and hide another in Manorbier."*

"I'll tell the warriors to go to Llawhaden shall I?" said Garibaldi.

"Yes, they must just ask permission to search for a fugitive, they're under orders not to disclose their real reason for searching the premises and grounds," instructed Tudor annoyed with Ivor too.

"We need to know about our enemies Ivor, what happened between you and Thomas Beckett?"

"It's foolish," sighed Ivor but continued, *"Slobbers was chosen as your Top Cat as we all know he has extraordinary powers. We elected for you to stay here as I'm training you, it made sense. And Slobbers lives here, it was the perfect choice. However, Thomas didn't approve and tried to elect himself and his equally intelligent cat, but he was ousted from the committee, and he lost his case. He got terribly upset and hasn't spoken to me since."*

"Apparently there is a sentry outside this castle, it would be very difficult to take a coracle inside without the guard asking questions," commented Elijas looking at Geraintus' notes.

"The Croggs would have had a plan if that's where it's hidden. Especially if they have befriended Thomas, knowing we've fallen out with him. It was well documented in the "Welsh Wizard weekly" that Thomas and I had had a feud concerning the magical Molly."

Molly was quietly beginning to lose faith in Ivor Llewellyn. She put it aside as Garibaldi returned to the table, with more Welsh cakes and tea.

"We need to decide about Carew Castle," said Elijas, *"The last few lines basically mean we must sell the chest, and we mustn't shed the first blood."*

"The chest is going tomorrow," said Gari, *"That's arranged."*

"No one must know we have this spoon. I'm going to visit Carew Castle, as Nesta, Helen of Wales may have more clues and historical information for us. In the meantime, ..."

The miners' lantern churned out green smoke at an alarming rate and before anyone could say anything, the second door in the secret passageway fell apart yet again as Garibaldi rushed towards it.

"Hi everyone," said Geraintus as he huffed, and he puffed as he slumped in a chair at the table. His green cape was torn, and his body were slightly charred, and he smelled of smoke.

"Whatever's happened to you?" asked Molly alarmed.

"It's the Begglys, the Croggs; they're burning down hutlets and houses that belong to the Llewellyn family. They're on their way to your castle Tudor and next is Harlech; we must inform Hopkin at once. They're searching for the spoon and seem to be setting fire to everything in sight."

"Are the Crogg brothers with them?" asked Ivor very uneasy in his chair.

"I don't know, I'm not sure, but there's pandemonium out there. We as head of the Llewellyn Empire need to act fast and do something."

"The soldiers on the beach have gone already, we can't send them," said Garibaldi hoping Molly wasn't going to send them to save Harlech castle or Tudors' even.

"Tudor go back to Caernarvon if you wish. We're staying here; it's a smoke screen. They want to distract us while they're hiding the coracle. I'm sure of it," said Molly.

"What about your house, where's the whispering fig tree?" asked Molly, as this was far more important.

"My house is in flames, I escaped in time. The tree is safe, but she needs moving. I'm going to need a location for her right away," said Geraintus still out of breath. Bedivere went to the kitchen and found some soothing potions as he administered them to Geraintus' left arm as it was shredded and needed a quick repair job.

"Robin and Rudge have also made comment that some of the Beggly armies seem to be heading in the direction of Carew Castle."

"*We need to defend Carew Molly,*" said Ivor gravely.

"*First blood will be at Carew then,*" said Molly as she swished her tail and left the table.

Outside, the dogs and cats were sat waiting for permission to enter. It was time to bury Gertrude, and a battle plan had to wait.

Chapter 18

The Croggs and the Golden Coracle again

With one coracle, the three brothers and the three Begglys moved swiftly towards their new location. It had been easy leaving the original coracle at Llawhaden Castle; Thomas Beckett hadn't been fazed at all.

Ali and Trent both knew there was something afoot, but neither of them discussed with each other. They both knew that Kentav was up to mischief, but neither of them wanted to get involved. Trent, however, was extremely pleased that Kentav wanted to include his girlfriend to assist in hiding the golden coracle.

They'd arrived at the church grounds of Manorbier Castle quite quickly and were waiting for Kentav to give his next instructions. Unbeknown to both Trent and Ali, the actual Golden Coracle had been hidden at Llawhaden. The coracle was full of their blankets and provisions; therefore, the brothers thought it was the real one.

Zupp, Zipp and Zapp had disappeared in all directions to ensure there was no enemy wandering around and more importantly, no Llewellyn's. They returned and Zupp whirled round to Kentav, his antennae spinning quite fast,

"Owain's men have passed through here today."

"We'll hide here, by these trees until Trent has made contact with Katrin, just in case."

Trent quickly disappeared from the churchyard and made his way towards the castle wall, knowing what his plan had been with Katrin. He could only hope that she'd not given up on them, as they'd detoured to Llawhaden. He was silently annoyed with Kentav but also pleased, as he'd asked Trent to help him hide the Golden Coracle. Trent had scurried down the slope as Kentav decided that this castle was quite hard to attack. Therefore, he was delighted with his decision to hide the decoy coracle here.

The castle itself was on a hill and it boasted impressive defensive turrets and bulwarks. Towards the western side of the castle, as it sloped down to the seaport, Kentav could see the advantage of hiding the coracle here. The southern side looked like the northern side it too had water under its walls, making infiltration by surprise quite impossible. There was another lake and the sweet flowing noise of a water mill that flowed through the valley below. The west side, the Severn Sea from Ireland entered a hollow bay, but this was some distance from the actual castle.

Kentav wondered where they'd be hiding the coracle.

"I might just live here once I'm Lord of the First Family of Wales; it's only a matter of time. This place is perfect," thought Kentav as they hid and waited for a signal from Trent.

It was a shame that Bevanuis wouldn't accept that he was a Crogg. Kentav liked him but didn't trust him as he knew, as did everyone else that Bevanuis spent more time with Geraldus than his own people. This was the predominant reason Kentav hadn't let the Golden Coracle be hidden here. Bevanuis was too much "in" with the Llewellyn's and not as seemingly loyal to the Croggs as he should. The last thing Kentav wanted was to lose the Coracle to the Llewellyn's. He couldn't fathom how Bevanuis was also allowing his brother to court his daughter as the Croggs, and the Llewellyn's didn't recognize marriages or courtships with each other.

He hadn't said a word to Trent as no -one apart from Kentav in the Crogg family knew that Bevanuis wasn't a Crogg. He was keeping this information to himself. Trent wasn't going to marry this girl anyway. Kentav didn't feel the need to tell him the secrets he was party too, which was why he was determined to get the treasure that he knew was his.

Zupp swept past Kentav and swiped down to inform him, what was going on at the front of the castle gates.

"Owain's men are at the castle gatehouse talking to Bevanuis. The footprints are different, they're not the same army, we saw in the fields."

"Stay here, all of you," instructed Kentav. *"We'll continue to hide until Trent has made contact. The men could be calling for any reason, there's a raging battle going on close to here. It could be nothing,"* said Kentav not worried. What really bothered him was that he hadn't seen any sign of Ivor Llewellyn. That troubled him more than anything. Something wasn't right. He knew that somewhere they would meet them; he could only hope that by then he'd hidden the Coracle.

***

Meanwhile, Katrin was getting extremely nervous indeed as she yet hadn't seen any sign from the churchyard to say that Trent had arrived. Katrin, who resembled her aunt, Kentav's wife had the customary gingery tuft at the front of her round head. She had freckles that covered her entire face, and her plump arms were also covered in gingery fair hair and freckles. She was quite tall for a Crogg, reaching five foot in her stocking feet. Thankfully, her figure was of hourglass perfection, which had attracted Trent towards her.

Katrin was also anxious, as she'd organised for the coracle to be hidden in the west wing of the castle, near her cousins' bedroom. However, since this plan, her mother had given the west side to her relatives who'd arrived unannounced yesterday. She hadn't a clue what she was going to do next. Trent Crogg had always been welcomed by her father but if he saw the other Croggs he would want to know why they were here. Her dad would also smell a nasty big rat and she'd be in trouble.

Trent was harmless and her father didn't mind him visiting.

She did know however, that her father didn't like Kentav Crogg and to see him here with his other brother, would cause chaos. Also, and unbeknown to poor Katrin her father had been building strong relations with the Llewellyn family, especially Owain and Geraldus.

Bevanuis had recognised a long time ago that it was best to be on the same side as the Llewellyn family. Bevanuis had never felt he was a Crogg in his whole life. Katrin didn't realise that through the impressive negotiating skills that her father possessed, they wouldn't be living here as a non-direct Llewellyn. All castles in Wales were historically only occupied by a Llewellyn family.

Owain Glyndwr had been so impressed with Bevanuis Williamus Crogg's skills as a negotiator during a war lord argument. This could have become a catastrophic problem for Owain and consequently, he'd allowed the Croggs to live in this castle temporarily. The outcome of the treasure findings would mean that the Llewellyn's would eventually reclaim the castle as theirs. This didn't really bother Bevanuis as he was so wrapped up helping the Llewellyn's that he believed he was one. As indeed he was, which was not common knowledge to anyone at this stage.

There was another difference between Bevanuis Crogg and the other family members. He didn't have the customary tuft of ginger hair, and he wasn't four feet. Bevanuis was a strapping six foot three without his fighting boots. He wore a slick black mop of hair and didn't resemble a Crogg at all. The only slight resemblance was the freckles on his arms and a few dotted on his nose. He'd always questioned his birth right and had discovered some of the family story that his mother had strayed.

He realised his father hadn't had any more children for that reason. He'd married his wife to keep up appearances and when Katrin had been born he'd distanced himself from her mother. He'd been devastated to watch his daughter grow up as a Crogg and not a Llewellyn. He'd battled with the knowledge of his family past, and he knew one day that the truth would prevail.

Katrin sat on the window ledge pondering where she should suggest they hide the Coracle. She gasped as she saw at least thirty of Owain's men outside the gatehouse with armour and horses. She observed them all going into the Castle as she heard the familiar noise of the wheel and chain of the drawbridge descending. The last thing she needed now was for Trent to turn up. Not only had her first plan been spoiled, but there were also soldiers in the castle and that was going to create an enormous problem. She would have to find out why they were here.

As she went to leave the window, she gasped again as she saw Trent's' signal from the orchard. Her heart sank, how was she going to help him now? This had been a stupid idea from the beginning. Whatever had possessed her to think that she could help?

She had to pass through the great hall towards the buttery and pantry to the servants' quarters where she was to meet Trent. She just hoped her father would be too pre-occupied with the soldiers to notice her slip past. She slid down the stairs as quiet as a mouse and tried not to think about this dilemma. She'd have to tell him, that it was impossible to hide the coracle at the castle with soldiers being entertained. She'd desperately wanted to help Trent restore some confidence with Kentav as he'd told her how much his brother had contempt for him.

Being over twenty and still unmarried she was eager to please Trent as she wanted him to fall in love and marry her. She would be an old maid if she weren't careful and with no siblings, she'd always felt isolated.

She heard raucous laughter downstairs in the hall and was relieved to witness they were all gathered around a map on the table and talking in groups. She smiled sweetly to herself as she hid behind the curtain and watched her father talking to Geraldus. Then she realised and went red in the face and became hot and bothered. She started to feel nauseous as she observed Geraldus and her father standing side by side talking intensely. It was obvious whereas it had never been apparent before. Her father looked like Geraldus' brother and not an ally; he was a Llewellyn.

She was now in an awful dilemma. The mission to help Trent riskier that she'd envisaged. These men would capture Trent and his brothers if they were seen on the premises; she'd no idea what to say to him. All she knew at that moment that the Coracle couldn't come into the Castle while the soldiers were there.

She scurried towards the back door, the servants not batting an eyelid. They all felt sorry for her, but all looked out for her too. They all felt she was wasting her time with Trent and made sure that her mother never found out what went on in her bedroom. Katrin wasn't an ugly duckling, but she wasn't exactly a princess either.

She wedged a stone against the back door, grabbed a cape from the peg on her way out. She shivered slightly as the breeze coming off the water caught her breath as she made her way down the slope towards the walled side gate.

Katrin didn't immediately see Trent but saw the puff of smoke from his pipe where he was hiding. She opened the gate and slid out and hurried towards him, he was hiding amongst the hazel trees.

Before Katrin could explain and offload what was going on, he saw her coming and smiled approvingly. She blushed a crimson orange making her freckles join up resembling orange peel as she hurried over to him.

"Katrin, my sweet pumpkin I'm so pleased to see you," whispered Trent in her ear and grabbed her tiny waist and held her tight.

Crushed by his hug and satisfied with this warm welcome gave Katrin an immediate sense of importance. She told Trent everything.

"Owain's' men are staying the night, Trent. It's all too risky."

"How come they're here, they were following us earlier or heading past us?"

"No, they're a different lot. I know they're staying, and with them here it's far too risky for you all to come into the castle."

"Yes, I know that. It's not your fault pumpkin. Kentav had us going to Llawhaden to hide a decoy coracle, that's why we're late," said Trent a little harshly then realised Katrin had shrunk back from his grasp. He was more concerned about Kentav's reaction; he would have a coronary when he relayed this news. However, Katrin got her composure back and said,

"I do have another plan, however. I've the spare key to the chamber under the Chapel, which is no longer in use. You can hide the coracle in there."

"Good, when can we bring it in and how do you propose we get it inside with Owain's men here, Katrin. This is crazy."

"In the morning, my mother is going out with my aunts and cousins and my father should be going out with the soldiers. When the drawbridge is down in the morning, you'll have ten minutes after the last party has ridden over the bridge, before the soldier lifts it again. That's your only chance."

"How do we get it out later once we've hidden it?" asked Trent knowing this was a disaster waiting to happen.

"I'll open the gates for you; the sentry will be at breakfast. I'll sort it out," said Katrin who sounded braver than she felt.

"I'll use my mirror to code you first thing; you'll need to stay in the churchyard. Get to those flowerbeds to the right of the drawbridge at dawn. Both parties should be leaving soon after. I will be inside waiting. Leave the sentry man to me."

"Right, I'll go and tell Kentav the plan. The bug dogs will be flying around just in case. We haven't seen any Llewellyn's yet and that's how we like it. Do you really think your dads' a Llewellyn?" asked Trent more concerned about this news than the coracle plan.

"Yes, it explains everything. Why Trent, will it affect us, what's wrong?"

Trent looked at her and realised in an instant it didn't matter if Katrin was a Crogg or a Llewellyn. At that moment he made his mind up and said nothing but smiled.

"Nothing is wrong my sweet pumpkin. Don't fret; I will see you in the morning. Let me go and calm Kentav down with the impossible task we have for him to hide his precious coracle. I'll see you first thing."

Katrin smiled and pushed a basket of Welsh cakes in his lap as he embraced her and they kissed for a long time, interrupted by a bug dog, swirling past hissing at them.

"Kentav apparently wants you back," whispered Katrin as Trent scurried away as quickly as he'd arrived.

Trent crept back to the church grounds knowing Kentav was going to go nuts. There was no other choice, it was his fault they'd gone to Llawhaden. It was Kentav's mess. He was not going to be a party to any of it, he'd decided.

***

Tucked in a secluded tree house, further down the orchard and invisible to the naked eye, were two absconded Croggs, Bethesda and Jethro. They had observed everything. Jethro had nearly fallen out of the tree house as Trent and Katrin had become passionate underneath the hazel tree, but it was time to send the information to the Llewellyn's. They could make out the coracle hidden under the trees with the Croggs in the churchyard and they had a full view of the gatehouse. Tomorrow was going to be interesting.

"Write the pebble Bethesda," said Jethro his right eye going round and round with embarrassment.

Jethro wrote the important pebble, tucked it in a silk pouch and swung it over the top branch of the tree. Within a second a flash of white light appeared, and the pebble disappeared to Ivor's cave.

⊷⟨✦⟩⊷

Chapter 19

Nesta of Wales.

Molly sat outside and observed her team of animals all patrolling the beach and realised that Ivor Llewellyn was hiding a few troubles of his own. She could understand as she'd her own demons and a mission to accomplish once she'd sourced this treasure. But she had a distinct feeling that Ivor's demons went much further. Garibaldi, who had been his aide forever, certainly wasn't about to inform them either, as that would be disloyal.

The general problem was evident in that there were too many old wizards trying to save their castles. It was time to do something. She would settle everyone down; give out the next instructions to the remaining warriors on the beach, who would soon march to Llawhaden. Once that was organised, she would visit Nesta, at Carew Castle. She needed to be sure; there was nothing missed from the riddle.

She knew the Croggs were winning in taking back the treasure which was not theirs to win. However, there was more to this hatred of the family than she'd been told. There was something deep rooted and amiss regarding the Croggs and so far, Ivor hadn't disclosed the entire family troubles.

She was also concerned about Garibaldi, who hadn't slept for days as when the Wizards were up, he had to be about, to deal with them. She knew what to do and went inside to speak with Hopkin immediately.

All the wizards were gathered round the table and the dogs were all on the hearth protecting the cushion, with the hidden spoon. Hopkin had disappeared to fetch his coach as Molly, without further ado, swished her tail over the whole cave, and muttered a sleep spell,

"Dimyngweld piwsagwyrdd / demand guhald peewsagweerdd," as she repeated it several times swishing her bushy tail all over the dining room.

The whole cave disappeared, leaving Molly standing on the step facing the beach. Harry the horse, brayed with approval as the ginger twins leapt on his back. They would still patrol the beach until she returned.

The oval pink coach glided towards her as Hopkin waved his hand and the glass steps threw themselves out of the door as the claws grabbed the sand for grip. She ran inside quickly, and the coach glided away as rapidly as it had arrived, leaving a sense of excitement with the twins and Harry.

Carew Castle wasn't too far from Saundersfoot as the coach skimmed the hedgerows on its way, cutting through Kilgetty towards Jeffreyston and then on to Carew. This had been discussed as the safest route avoiding the coastal roads and assuming the Croggs were all in the Manorbier area.

Carew Castle had a mill pond, which again matched the clues in terms of water with a tidal mill, very much a favourite piece of working machinery at the castle. Nesta's husband, who was fighting with Owain, also called Gerald had purchased the castle for her. Therefore, this castle was already in ownership with an AP Llewellyn, giving Molly no reason apart from being curious, to visit.

Nesta was a sick lady, however. The locals called her "*the white lady of Carew Castle.*" She was dreadfully unhappy with the current situation, which she could do nothing about. Her husband had been away for a long time fighting and the worry was taking its toll on her health.

A crystal pebble had been sent in advance to warn her and Molly hoped that this might cheer her up. To have visitors at her Castle, as she was spending an immense amount of time on her own, waiting for Gerald to come home; should have been a good thing.

The coach descended and came to a halt as it landed on the grounds directly opposite the north tower. The castle was breath-taking in size and stature and was as impressive as Hopkin had explained on their journey.

Hopkin waved his hand sending dozens of little harps from his triple cuffed cloak towards the coach as he muttered a spell for it to disappear. Molly smiled as these actions always made her feel aware of how magical all the wizards were, even though their capabilities were dwindling.

Nesta appeared at the top step of the side entrance, dressed in white and looked more frightened than pleased to see them.

"Please, welcome, come in," she whispered barely taking a breath as she turned, and Hopkin and Molly moved quickly up the steps behind her.

"She looks as if she's seen a ghost," thought Molly as Hopkin looked at her and agreed.

Nesta waved her hand towards the window seat overlooking the mill pond as she went to sit opposite and asked,

"How can I help you both?"

"We're in search of the Golden Coracle, Nesta. You were mentioned in the riddle, given to us at Talley Lakes. We thought you might have a clue for us?" said Hopkin quietly as it was obvious that Nesta wasn't herself.

"There are so many rumours going round to your task in hand," said Nesta vaguely.

"Really, can you explain?" said Hopkin.

"There were men here the other day, waiting for Owain as usual. While they were getting ready, they were talking about seeing some Croggs camping in a field with two coracles. They would have intercepted them, but they were late meeting Owain's troops, so they left them alone."

"Did any of them have an idea where the Croggs were headed with two coracles?" asked Molly holding her breath for a moment hoping for another clue.

"No, I don't know anything else. Let's eat," said Nesta moving towards a table in the far corner of the room which had a buffet prepared for their arrival.

"Thank you," said Molly as they walked to the table.

"I'd love to show Molly your beautiful gardens before we leave, may I?" asked Hopkin devouring a drumstick of chicken as he talked and winked at Molly at the same time.

The caldron steaming in the fireplace seemed to give out an aura of knowledge and Molly ate thinking of the riddle and listening to Hopkin and Nesta chatter away. She relaxed very quickly with Hopkin. Molly kept thinking of the poem, *"Nesta, Helen of Wales, says it's true."* At least Molly knew she was true regarding the men, but Molly also knew somehow there must be something else as she patiently continued listening to Nesta's chatter.

"We had to cover the wishing well last week."

Molly's ears pricked up and Hopkin looked at her as she gulped her drink and composed herself quickly as Hopkin asked,

"Why, what happened?"

All Molly could think, was the other line of the riddle, *"Find the clue, an ancient place with wishing well,"* as she held her breath waiting for Nesta to explain.

"The well was making noises and screeching throughout the night as if someone were upsetting it. The servants were kept awake and eventually before

Gerald left, he had it filled in with earth and dung from the horses."

"*Has this worked?"* asked Molly trying to act normal.

"*Oh yes, we haven't heard a peep from it since. We have no idea why it started screeching in the first place."*

This was a serious clue as Hopkin and Molly exchanged glances over the table as Nesta kept chattering, now visibly enjoying her guests.

"*Can we take a look at it?"* asked Molly now feeling an urgent sense of something important.

"*Well, there's not much to see; it's a mound of earth,"* said Nesta.

"*We need to see it, Nesta. The wailing has coincided with Molly's arrival and the coracle and spoon being stolen from us, even though we won the battle,"* said Hopkin. He was also mindful that an absent-minded sick lady might talk out of turn to the servants, without realising it.

"*You mean there might be a message inside for you?"*

"*Possibly,"* said both Molly and Hopkin together.

"*Why didn't you answer Garibaldi's' pebble about wishing wells?"* asked Hopkin out of interest as he tried to contain his excitement.

"*I was too upset to bother I'm sorry. The well had given us so many sleepless nights and trouble, the last thing I wanted was for anyone to know we even had a well. I didn't realise the question may help the Llewellyn family. You must forgive me,"* said Nesta humbled as she bowed her head. She got up from the table and beckoned for Hopkin and Molly to follow her. She realised she shouldn't have ignored a pebble from the Llewellyn's and Gerald would have a fit if he discovered her bad manners.

"We're here now, that's all that matters," said Molly forgiving her immediately and growing excited with the anticipation of seeing the covered well.

They were both excited and anxious at the same time as they descended the stairs following an eager Nesta, who felt their excitement.

They arrived at a mound of dung which stank and looked like a massive beehive. The stench was unbearable as Nesta excused herself, as the dung gave her an instant headache. She apologised for her tardiness and stepped back away from Hopkin and Molly, as they stood staring at the stinking mound in front of them.

"I can change this," said Molly as she swished her tail in the air and spun it round chanting,

"Beniali, benialli," she repeated three times. The dung heap collapsed and became a flower bed full of snowdrops and daffodils; however, it still covered the well entirely.

"Now we need the flowers to disappear," suggested Hopkin as he guided her through her spells.

"*Gemblali beillioni,*" she repeated three times swishing her tail in the opposite direction releasing angel dust from her tail.

The wailing began immediately as the well was restored to its original form. The screeching got louder by the second and it was coming from the centre. Nesta, who'd stayed a bit further back, slapped her hand over her ears and ran to the steps to the tower. She couldn't bear any of it and left Hopkin and Molly to deal with it.

"*We need to look inside Hopkin,*" said Molly not bothered by the high-pitched screeching. "*Maybe there's a clue inside.*"

They both peered over the edge and couldn't see anything as it was pitch black, but the noise was coming from the centre of the well, deep inside.

"*Hopkin make me a rope and I'll have a look. I can tie my tail to it.*"

Hopkin didn't waste time and within a second a pink cloud arrived, and a twenty-foot rope appeared from nowhere.

Molly grabbed the end of the rope and attached her tail and secured it with a splattering of angel dust. Hopkin muttered a spell, and an oak tree grew from the side of the well, which he secured the rope around.

"*I'll use the tree to help me drop you slowly, Molly.*"

Hopkin held the rope around his waist and his hands, knowing the tree was keeping them secure. Molly clambered down the side, the wailing continued at full decibels. Molly disappeared as Hopkin gently let the rope move inch by inch as her tail disappeared. The second she disappeared the wailing stopped as Hopkin suddenly looked visibly shocked.

"Molly, come back, it's too dangerous," shouted Hopkin as he pulled the rope back and moved towards the edge of the well. Something was wrong; he pulled the rope back up but no Molly.

Hopkin stood there mangled with a rope around his torso and had a dreadful feeling in the pit of his stomach. It was the worst time of Hopkin Paulinus' life. He'd never lost a family member before and he'd never had a spell go wrong in his entire lifetime, as he tried everything in his power, to bring Molly back from the darkness.

He tried all his *"pink spells,"* his *"three feathers' spells,"* even his *"thearasaurus in times of emergency spells,"* but nothing.

Absolutely nothing at all.

An hour had gone by, and the silence was now much worse than the wailing. This situation was disastrous, he couldn't leave Molly here, in the well. The pink coach would soon arrive to take them back to the cave. The cave had been spelled with a sleeping draught; he had to return to protect it. Otherwise, the family along with the Hugglett spoon would be vulnerable to the enemy.

He continued to murmur every spell he knew as the rope had slowly disappeared round the oak tree; the tree had shrunk to the ground. Everything looked the same, but the well was quiet. The purring in the distance of his oval coach broke his concentration as he tried to bring Molly back.

He was distraught and alighted the steps to the coach, not bothering to say goodbye to Nesta. She wouldn't remember much. All Hopkin could think about as the coach whirled round the estate towards Saundersfoot was the Llewellyn family. How could he walk into Ivor's cave and tell them that Molly had drowned in the well, never to be heard of or seen since her investigation?

His stomach churned, he felt sick, and this was the worst day of his life. He was an expert in spells, and he couldn't think what he was going to say. There was no point pretending, he had failed. The expert wizard and head of the family had got it wrong.

The coach flew quicker than normal, sensing Hopkin's unease. All Hopkin could think about was that wretched line in the poem, *"Death is imminent for a friend; not foe."* He only hoped this didn't mean the Magical Molly, surely not.

The coach landed on the beach, and he gathered himself together to unlock the spell. He nearly missed the step and fell over as he realised the cave was in full view, with lights on, everything appeared normal.

He walked towards the cave, the animals greeting him as if there was no imminent disaster afoot, which was strange. Wibbly Alf greeted him at the front door as he walked in. His heart was in his stomach, dreading the moment he had to tell them all.

"At last Hopkin, we were wondering how long you'd be. I've news of significant importance," smiled Molly as Garibaldi appeared from the kitchen with a plate full of Welsh cakes and a large teapot full of unique tea. *"Come and sit, we have lots to discuss."*

Hopkin smiled uncontrollably; his relief evident to Ivor who nodded with understanding as he plonked himself in a coracle chair. He knew she was magical, but he hadn't realised she was *this* magical......

Chapter 20

The Golden Eagles

Suddenly there was pandemonium inside the cave as it dawned on everyone that Molly, who'd arrived and spelled the cave back to normal, had returned without Hopkin. Hopkin, who was as white as a sheet still from the mere thought, that they'd lost Molly, was stunned and speechless.

Rat tat tat

The goose dropped a crystal pebble at Wibbly's feet who raced it round to Garibaldi before anyone could say anything about Molly's comments and Hopkins' state of hypnotism.

"Ah, a pebble from Bethesda and Jethro," said Garibaldi as he read it quickly before saying it aloud. Everyone inside the cave was silent.

"All three Croggs hiding in Cemetery; one coracle, three Beggly bugs and an army of Owain's' men here overnight. They're not the same ones from the beach. Will Pebble once coracle moves. B&J."

"Different men, Geraldus and Bevanuis are together then," said Tudor.

"How do you know that Tudor?" said Ivor a bit too quickly, as he knew the truth.

"*You know as well as I do, that Bevanuis is our half-brother and Geraldus is his brother. It won't be long before one of the Croggs discovers this fact unless they know already.*"

"*What difference does this make to our next plan?*" asked Molly getting as confused as the others listening. She had revelations to share with everyone and the pebble had distracted them.

"*Tudor has a point,*" said Hopkin. "*If the Croggs know this, they wouldn't drag a magical coracle they've just stolen to Manorbier Castle. The family could defect to us immediately; therefore, the coracle they're going to hide in Manorbier is the fake one. I would imagine Kentav Crogg knows a lot more than we've given him credit.*"

"*Do you think they know, as this is quite a significant piece of family information, you're now disclosing?*" said Molly beginning to get very annoyed with Ivor.

"*I would think Kentav knows,*" said Garibaldi quietly.

"*I agree with Garibaldi, Kentav is far more knowledgeable about our past than he's been given credit,*" said Hopkin as Ivor visibly flinched at his words.

"*This eliminates our dilemma then,*" said Molly. "*We have men going to Llawhaden to look for the coracle as we speak. We must go and help them find it. If Robin and Rudge hadn't messaged us to say there were two, we wouldn't have known. They've left the Golden Coracle with Beckett for safe keeping and have taken the fake to Manorbier. It now makes sense.*"

Yo-Yo, Slobbers, and the dogs were huddled near the fireplace listening, the spoon tucked inside the cushion amongst them. They knew an adventure was imminent and they all wanted a piece of the action. Wibbly Alf, who was positioned outside, had come in and was sat with the door to his back, also listening.

"Can you send a feather bound pebble to Thomas Beckett, Ivor? Ask him if he can accommodate you for the night?" asked Molly.

"Well, I don't know as we fell out because I told him that my cat was better than his. This was as I said before you came, we haven't talked since," said Ivor who realised he'd been a stubborn fool.

"He didn't reply to the pebble when we sent it asking about the wishing well either," said Bedivere.

"Maybe he knew he had the coracle and didn't want to get involved," said Tudor.

"No," said Molly. *"I don't think he knows it's been hidden there, or if it's been left there, he doesn't know it's the Golden Coracle. The Croggs may have said, they were leaving a coracle with him, but I doubt they'd tell him, it's our treasure, whether he's a fair-weather family member or not."*

"His cat would have pebbled me anyway," chipped in Slobbers, as they all turned to listen to him.

"What makes you say that Slobbers?" said Garibaldi not wishing his Top Cat to look foolish in front of the great Hopkin Paulinus.

"He likes to be important and whenever the Warriors have been over there, he always tells me. I could pebble him and pretend to ask for his help. I'll be coming with Ivor," suggested Slobbers wanting to be in on the action.

"Good, Slobbers send a pebble to the cat, whatever his name is. Ivor, I suggest you pebble Thomas, ask for his forgiveness and that you're coming to see him, as you're passing and could you stay the night?" said Molly, as Ivor went a bright scarlet but nodded.

"Gari, can you make some more tea while I change into my night collar."

As soon as Molly left the room, the animals started to squabble on who was going with Slobbers.

"I'm coming with you," said Yo-Yo.

"You can't," retorted Millie from the hearth. *"You're in complete charge of the Hugglett spoon; you can't go anywhere."*

Wibbly Alf puffed out his big white and chocolate coloured chest and went to Millie, *"We shall go with Slobbers instead."*

"No, I'm top dog and Slobbers and I will go," insisted Yo-Yo getting quite exasperated by his new responsibility which he felt was now holding him back from helping the Magical Molly.

"I'll decide in a moment everyone what's best," said Molly on her return.

"Gari, send a coal pebble to the warriors on their way to Llawhaden. Tell them what they're looking for,

but to leave whether they've seen it or not and let us know. We will deal with it once Ivor gets there," said Molly, as everyone realised, she had the full picture of the riddle. Yet she hadn't had chance to disclose what had happened to her from the wishing well.

"I need to explain to you all, especially to Hopkin, what happened to me at Carew Castle earlier," said Molly needing everyone's attention.

Rat tat tat.

"That was quick," said Elijas, who was in awe of them all, for a change.

"Two pebbles, one for Slobbers and one for Garibaldi," said Ginger Two as he placed them on the table and went outside to keep watch as Wibbly engaged in the goings on.

"What did Beckett say, Gari?" asked Ivor hoping he hadn't lost his friendship with Beckett just because he was more important than him.

"He says, "Come along when it pleases you,"" said Garibaldi reading aloud.

"What does mine say, Gari?" asked Slobbers enthusiastically feeling important right now.

"See you soon, fat cat," said Gari and he immediately wished he hadn't. Slobbers' great big tail fell to the floor in embarrassment as Molly soothed over it quickly,

"Slobbers, you're a great big cat, you can go with Ivor as you're now expected. The rest of us will need to

plan how we're going to seek out the coracle if Owain's' men don't find the whereabouts of it first."

"Surely, we need to wait for the warrior's pebble before Ivor and Slobbers leave," said Geraintus, who'd been quiet up till now.

"What happened to you earlier, Molly?" asked Elijas who was dying to know, and everyone was forgetting that she knew everything.

"Yes Geraintus, we'll wait for the information from the men, but the next part of our challenge is much harder," said Molly not making sense as she sat back in her chair and explained,

"When Hopkin helped me down into the well it was quite eerie. The bottom itself was covered in a liquid substance, like silvery water. I touched it with my paw, and it dragged me underneath. I thought I was drowning but within seconds, I found myself in a cavern where it was pitch dark, but with specks of gold glistening within the walls."

"Where were you?" asked Hopkin although he was now back to normal after his shock but realised what Molly was about to say and smiled.

"Ivor, you mentioned before I arrived and a long time ago, about your third cousin removed, Ivor AP Meurig," as Ivor nodded.

"He oversaw looking after the Golden Treasure chest, the one we need. Owain's lot wanted him to go to war and he summoned two of his best soldiers to

watch over the treasure, our treasure until his return. He transformed them into Golden Eagles, to protect this treasure and......."

"Eagles are coming; red kites or bats no," quoted Bedivere slightly interrupting Ivor as Molly continued.

"Goodness....is?"

"Ivor let her finish, for goodness' sake," interrupted Tudor.

"You were a long time, what happened exactly?" asked Hopkin wanting all the detail.

"I found myself in the gold dust cavern where it is dark, cold, and very damp and smelly. I could about make out the treasure chest glistening in the corner. I was not in the silvery water, but on the side near the small entrance. The dim light was enough for me to see the chest. It has gold bullion padlocks all over it and covered in gold chains, as thick as Wibbly's link chain. I went to try to open it and as soon as I got close, I was attacked by one of the two Eagles, who pinned me to the ground."

"What happened, how did you survive," asked Elijas, who was now paying attention as historically everyone knew the Golden Eagles at this castle had killed many a predator and enemy.

"I murmured our last plea for help spell, which all our wizards know Elijas," said Molly.

"All of you guys need to remember it while we're talking about it," said Molly, *"It's **Vitagliano/ pagliettini**." It will give you three seconds to get away*

from imminent danger and make yourselves invisible or disappear. Otherwise, you'll die."

"What happened next?" asked Slobbers who'd come closer.

"I kept murmuring the spell and one of the Eagles recognised it and stopped the other one from attacking me. It had me pinned on the ground. He was about to sink his golden talons into me. But the second Eagle, who was protecting the entrance realised who I was, and ordered his colleague from me. I kept murmuring the spell, which made them both stop. They spent the next few minutes explaining their situation and their master has been killed fighting. We need to help them once we get the ...."

"Ivor AP Meurig has been killed?" asked Ivor going quite ashen in colour and interrupting Molly.

"Ivor, that can wait, Molly tell us everything," said Tudor frustrated with Ivor.

"All out papers are in this chest, which is why they were tasked to protect it. If we haven't enough evidence of our standard and apart from winning the battle, we have proof inside the chest," said Molly.

"Goodness me, why didn't Ivor AP Meurig tell me this?" said Ivor quietly disturbed about something.

"For precisely the same reasons you are withholding family history from us Ivor," retorted Molly as she continued to explain.

Garibaldi looked at Hopkin and they both nodded, they knew that Molly would soon decipher all of Ivor's demons, given the chance.

"So, the treasure chest is already there?" said a bewildered Elijas.

"Yes, we need to take our coracle there for it to link up with the spoon, which will be attached to it by Wibbly's link chain. There is no entrance to the cavern from the castle grounds only a very narrow path and the entrance to the cavern is about four foot high. The important thing is, we only need the coracle, and we all need to get to Castell Coch where we shall assume residence."

"We can't open the gates until the spoon is attached to the coracle," said Ivor.

"We can fly over the walls in our coaches, Ivor. There's nothing we can't do. We might be diminishing in powers, but we can still rustle up a plan to get the treasures together," said Bedivere getting quite excited as indeed everyone else started to feel the euphoria already.

"We need to remember that we mustn't fall into the silvery watery substance in the cavern. It will take you under, drown you and send the wishing well at Carew Castle, into a wailing mode alerting enemies in the area," explained Molly.

"I spelled it back to the dung heap Molly before I left, to be sure," said Hopkin pleased he hadn't lost all his faculties.

"There is no doubt the substance is a killer, I don't know how I survived it, but the Eagles have killed numerous predators just by throwing them into the murky water. This is the Eagles telling me, more than knowledge on my part," said Molly.

"How do the Eagles get restored back to men if Ivor AP Meurig is dead?" asked Elijas beginning to believe these wizards really did have powers.

"There will be instructions in the chest, Elijas," said Ivor knowing he needed to get to the chest to see what other papers were in there.

"What else is in the chest, Ivor?" asked Molly sensing there were unmentioned secrets or treasures being talked about in the room, but no wizard were saying anything. Molly knew that every time Garibaldi disappeared to the kitchen with the teapot, something was being avoided or Ivor was not telling the truth.

Molly realised that Ivor had something to hide but didn't want to tackle him until all the treasures were together, and then she would want to know everything.

"We've solved the riddle. We need to bring the coracle to Carew and then unlock the chest, link the spoon and we should have all our powers restored," said Ivor visibly relieved.

"We're far from solving how we're going to get the real coracle away from Llawhaden yet Ivor," said Hopkin taking a Welsh cake from the slate plate on the table and took a mug of tea from Garibaldi.

"Yes, I know........"

Rat tat tat.

Wibbly Alf opened the door and Ginger One appeared with a return pebble and gave it to Garibaldi. He read it carefully as everyone sat silenced by the anticipation, they were close now.

"It's from the men at Llawhaden Castle, it says "No coracle anywhere, but two locked dungeons with no apparent available keys. Will position around perimeter and await instructions.""

"It's got to be there," said Molly. *"What's the name of the cat, Slobbers?"*

"Fat Cat," said Slobbers as all the animals listening chuckled. *"He was never named officially so he became fat cat. He calls me fat cat as a sort of joke. I can ask for his help when we get there. Ivor can talk to Beckett while we both explore the dungeons. When do we leave?"*

"He'll smell a rat, surely?" said Bedivere.

"Fat cat has no loyalty to Beckett, I know from the things he says," said Slobbers, *"I know how to manage him."*

"Good, that's sorted then, Ivor go and take some sleep as you'll be decoy whilst the rest of us steal back the coracle," instructed Molly as Ivor got up, didn't need to be told twice. Garibaldi followed him and gave him a sleeping draught knowing Ivor wasn't in favour with anyone right now. He really must come clean and tell Molly and the others his darkest secrets. Garibaldi

sighed, they would have to wait, but he felt slightly at fault too, as he hadn't said anything either.......maybe he should.

"First things first Gari," said Molly as Garibaldi returned to the dining room. *"Send a pebble to the men at Llawhaden and inform them that we'll take it from there."*

"If we're all seen going to Llawhaden then the Croggs will turn up and pretend to fight for the coracle," said Bedivere.

"We need to get Yo-Yo to Castell Coch first, to be sure we have two of the sacred treasures in the same place," suggested Hopkin.

"Yes," said Molly in tune with this wizard, *"We also need Millie and Wibbly, who seem to have linked collars, especially Wibbly's link chain with us when we find the coracle."*

"We need the Ginger twins to determine if the Croggs are still at Manorbier," said Bedivere.

"No, why don't I go back to the whispering fig tree and instruct Robin and Rudge to fly over and find out?" said Geraintus.

"That's wasting time, why don't we send Bethesda and Jethro a pebble asking for an urgent update. We need to get going on this information," said Elijas beginning to get bored with it all.

"That's a better plan, of course," said Molly quite surprised that Bediveres' friend was taking some interest in the whole treasure hunt at last.

"You need to fetch the tree Geraintus and take it to Castell Coch. We need to set up our base camp there. Once we leave here, we will flatten this cave once we've moved into Castell Coch."

Garibaldi nearly dropped the teapot he was carrying as no one had discussed this with him!

"Molly's right Gari. This cave is too vulnerable, and we need to move our living accommodation to suit our new status," said Hopkin. *"I'll continue to live in Harlech, and Tudor will stay in Caernarvon, there will be plenty of castles to distribute when we have all the treasures together."*

"Geraintus, tackle the tree and take it to Coch, we will be there shortly. We shall leave once we hear from Bethesda and Jethro."

Geraintus disappeared through the secret passageway, leaving a trail of green smoke lingering in the dining room.

"We must remember we may have spies outside," said Bedivere looking through all the notes to date.

"Yes, especially if we all leave after Slobbers and Ivor have departed, we must keep Harry here with the twins and make the place look busy," said Hopkin.

"Where are we all going?" asked Wibbly, who knew he was going with Millie, but Molly wasn't clear yet.

Rat tat tat.

Goose entered this time with two more pebbles and placed them in Wibbly's paw, Millie went to sit at the door while Wibbly dropped them at Garibaldi's' feet.

"What do they say, Gari?" asked Slobbers keen to get on with his mission.

"First one is Owain's' men, "Moving out as requested, two dungeons, no keys.""

"And the other?"

"Croggs on the move and Coracle inside castle. We'll be at Manorbier house, our sisters' residence if required; let us know. B&J"

"Right," said Molly, *"Slobbers get ready, Garibaldi wake Ivor, he needs to get going to Llawhaden Castle immediately. Hopkin, fetch the pink coach and prepare them to fly in half an hour."*

"We could do with finding out where the Croggs are headed," said Hopkin as he prepared to summon his coach.

As Hopkin mentioned the Croggs, the lantern in the hallway started to rumble and turned black, the froth cascading out of its sides flowing into the dining room. The chandelier above the table began to rustle and twinkle, the thimble tips turning black as the room went cold.

"What's going on?" shouted Elijas as Bedivere got up to re-spell the lantern. Ivor walked in, fully robed for his journey, and turned ashen as the black smoke swirled around him, the animals at the hearth beginning to panic.

"No one moves," instructed Molly as she looked at Hopkin.

The front door swung open as Bedivere, and Garibaldi calmed the lantern and chandelier. Hopkin sent Molly a message through her tail as she acknowledged the information. Ginger Two was shouting,

"They're coming this way, hundreds of them......"

*Crash......*the secret passageway fell apart.

"Oh, my goodness, we're under attack," shouted Elijas as Bedivere waved his hand over him making him shut up at once.

Geraintus was a deeper green than normal and was panting....

*"The Croggs are on their way, there's a full army but only two brothers, and you've got 'till morning before they get to the main beach. I must get back to sort the tree...."*as he left as quickly as he'd arrived.

"Hopkin summon the three feathers coach. Ivor and Slobbers get the pink one. Everyone we need to leave; this is what we'll do," instructed Molly shaking her tail in the air restoring calm around her as the animals huddled together with the cushion amongst them. Ivor and Slobbers followed Hopkin and Garibaldi started packing the relevant information that was strewn across the dining room and table.

Chapter 21

The Croggs hunt for the Hugglett spoon.

For all his faults and he had many, Kentav did recognise that Trent looked scared as he scurried back to the churchyard to report back. It was evident that there was a flaw in the plan as Kentav listened to Trent.

"Who are the men then?" asked Ali a bit more worried than Kentav, he didn't like the sound of this so-called plan at all.

"Don't be hasty Ali," said Kentav trying to look a bit brotherlike than he felt. He needed both of them right now and after he was ensconced in the castle, he would dispose of them.

Ali surprised with Kentav's calmness closed his mouth with shock.

"It's not Trent's fault that Katrin has had to change the original plan. I'm sure the chapel dungeon is fine. The tricky bit is going over the drawbridge at dawn. I'm sure it's under control, there nothing we can do about it. It's not his fault, Ali."

Trent surprised but pleased that Kentav was supportive grew in stature feeling important,

"We'll move towards the stand of trees before dawn. Once the drawbridge opens and the soldiers leave, we wait and once the family leave, we will hear a blast of a horn. We have one minute to get inside before the drawbridge goes back up. We've enough time; Katrin is going to distract the sentry over the turret. It should work," he said sounding more confident than he felt.

"Ok Begglys, fetch some frogs or worms for us to make supper. We might as well camp quietly here until dawn. Well done, Trent," said Kentav graciously which made Ali smell even more of a big rat.

Ali sorted out the blankets in the coracle but didn't get to the bottom of the pile otherwise he would have seen it wasn't the Golden one. He was in deep thought thinking that Kentav was up to no good and was of course using him and his brother, as he always did.

ZUPPPPPPPPPPPP.

The main bug dog whirled to a halt at Kentav's feet.

"We've spies on the trees in the orchard, there's a cloud formation," zapped Zupp head bug dog, his antennae swirling round making Trent feel quite sick. He hated these things.

"Where are they, do you know who they are?" asked Ali an uneasy feeling creeping into his voice as Kentav felt the same unease. He knew it had been too good to be true, not seeing any Llewellyn's. He may have trained them, but he had a quiet dislike for them.

"No idea," said Zupp as he continued swirling round them, the other two bugs patrolling their perimeter to be safe.

"Could be just a cloud Kentav," said Ali knowing it wasn't.

"We haven't seen any wizards, let's be fair Kentav. We've got away with taking the coracle, now hiding it and we haven't seen any sight of them, till now if it's them," said Trent.

"I agree," said Ali, *"I'm amazed we've not been ambushed."*

"That's what worries me," said Kentav for the first time being honest. He was bothered now; the brothers were right. They'd not seen or heard of the Wizards; it was very odd that Ivor Llewellyn hadn't marched his men to the factory and demanded he returned the coracle. Not a whisper from them, no fight for the coracle, it was making Kentav a little afraid. There could be an ambush inside the castle.

"Are you sure Katrin is on our side Trent and that the men are leaving in the morning?"

"Yes definitely, they've got a battle brewing with Owain Glyndwr. Katrin heard it plainly as she was spying on them in the hall," said Trent annoyed that Kentav doubted his sweet Katrin.

"Shall I zap them from the tree and kill them?" said Bug dog two waiting instructions, his antennae whirling round.

"*No,*" said Kentav, "*Let them see us deliver the coracle to the castle. We'll go to Ivor's cave after this and demand the spoon. It's time,*" said Kentav to Ali's horror as Trent went paler than usual. Neither of them wanted confrontation and Ali quietly decided there and then that he was going to go home and pack his bags and leave for distant lands. He didn't want anything to do with this; he knew deep down that the treasure didn't belong to them.

Trent was equally mortified with this statement. He had also quietly decided that he would marry Katrin and stay in the castle that was his only way out.

"*Let's camp down, bug dogs, keep watch. Whoever is spying on the castle can watch us hide the coracle at dawn, perfect,*" smiled Kentav thinking he was ahead of them.

***

Bethesda and Jethro were very cramped in their little tree house but pleased they hadn't been spotted so far. The cloud above them looked like a water cloud about to burst and it wasn't apparent to the naked eye.

"*Get some sleep Jethro, I shall wake you if something happens before dawn,*" said Bethesda enjoying his spying mission.

"*Yes ok,*" said Jethro as he shut his eye, the black one not closing but moving round and round making Bethesda uncomfortable as in the dark it looked even more gruesome than usual.

The sun started to rise and suddenly the drawbridge clanked loudly as Bethesda nudged Jethro to wake up. The drawbridge descended to the ground covering the moat as a harass of horses cantered out. The horses were swathed in purple, with eye protection and armour. Geraintus and Bevanuis led the soldiers away, the standard of the Llewellyn crest, the candle, and the moon evident as Bethesda and Jethro gasped in awe of the sight beneath them. The four horses behind the leaders were adorned with turquoise and this would have confirmed the Llewellyn insignia to anyone in doubt regarding the Llewellyn colours and standard.

The horses disappeared quickly past the cemetery and Kentav felt sick. His anger rose even further as he watched the horses pass them. He knew this indeed was the Llewellyn standard and he'd no right to question it. This made him even more furious as he realised that this was what he had wanted all along. To be Lord of the Castles and in command.

Ali could sense Kentav's anger and realised the sooner he went home after this, the better. He needed to leave for distant lands immediately. He'd seen Kentav in this frame of mind before and at that time he'd killed his own flesh and blood.

Trent also watched Kentav, knowing they hadn't a chance against those soldiers on horses, even the family were not a match for them. His decision to stay in the castle and marry Katrin was firmly in his mind. He also remembered what Kentav was capable of if his blood started to boil. His growing red face currently watching the horses canter pass was a sure sign.

Stealing coracle

"Quick, we need to get to the line of trees, we'll only have a minute," whispered Trent as Kentav stood motionless after witnessing the sight of the soldiers.

"Kentav snap out of it right now, for goodness' sake," whispered Ali as he started to move deftly and followed Trent to the line of trees.

Bethesda and Jethro watched in silence above them, waiting for the coracle to be taken inside before pebbling Ivor.

Eventually, a scream of laughter emerged from the castle and six horses appeared with glamorous ladies astride each one. They could be heard giggling as they trotted over the drawbridge oblivious to anyone around them. They were off to Pembroke on a lady outing, and no one had bothered to ask Katrin if she'd wanted to join them. No one asked Katrin much these days, she observed sadly.

The ladies disappeared as quickly as the soldiers over the hill and suddenly Kentav felt nervous.

"Your call Trent," he whispered to the tree line.

"Quick, let's go," he commanded as they scurried quickly over the drawbridge. A klaxon sounded as they disappeared through the gates as the drawbridge slowly stared to rise.

"That was close," whispered Katrin in the shadows as she beckoned for them all to move to the chapel side immediately.

She opened a side door, the entrance to the chapel and the kitchens which were no longer in use. They were puffing quite hard as they dragged the coracle along the very dry grass to the door.

"*Hurry,*" whispered Katrin anxious the sentry above may just look down at any time and observe their goings on.

"*All right,*" shouted Kentav suddenly angry at this whole situation. He was not going to let the Llewellyn's get away with this treasure. He was even angrier when they arrived at the side door as the door was too small for the coracle.

"*It's too big for the door,*" said Ali suddenly and smiled as he could see Kentav was now in a fix. How was he going to get away with hiding the fake one? He'd known all along; this was going to be interesting.

"*Turn it on its side, and then it will fit,*" said Trent. Kentav looked on in horror knowing the blanket covering the coracle would fall out and everyone would see it wasn't the Golden Coracle.

Ali suddenly got some extra strength and wanted to expose Kentav, who had no chance of protesting as they all lifted the coracle to its side. Immediately the blanket uncovered the coracle as they moved it inside the chapel.

Kentav realised that no one would really know but to his utmost horror the look on Katrin's face told him otherwise. Her face displayed shock and surprise all at once, even Trent noticed.

Katrin had read all about the Golden Coracle from their library information at the castle. It was common knowledge that the coracle had been missing all these years and the detail that surrounded the coracle was well documented. This wasn't it.

She looked inside the coracle and registered the ash seat was missing, the link chain wasn't attached, and she went a bright orange as she knew this was a fake. She looked Kentav straight in the eye but didn't say a word.

Ali noticed first and didn't say anything either as all he wanted was to leave and not get into an argument inside someone else's castle.

"Let's go," said Ali as he didn't want confrontation.

"This way," said Katrin pleased no one had said anything. They all followed Katrin as they dragged the fake coracle and placed it in the dungeon, which Katrin secured and gave Trent the key.

"I'm staying here," said Trent, it was time to part company with Kentav.

Kentav went berserk.

"No, you're coming with us, we're going to the Llewellyn's today, it's time. The bug dog army are waiting for us on route back, we're going to challenge them for the spoon, you must come," shouted Kentav. The sight of the horses in their splendour had angered him to the point of extreme jealousy and hatred.

"Sorry, Kentav. I've done my bit and I've no intention of leaving here until I ask Katrin's father for her hand in marriage. I'll follow you once I've had permission."

Katrin went bright orange again, and with pleasure. She forgot for a moment they were standing around a fake coracle.

"Very well Trent, don't expect a bloody castle when I've all the treasures in my possession and I'm Lord of the Kingdom," shouted Kentav furious with both brothers.

Ali decided to intervene for the first time and the last time, unbeknown to Ali.

"This is not the Golden Coracle Kentav. You know it and you've dragged Katrin into this mess and made Trent and I look fools. What's really going on? Is there something about this family that we're not aware of? Why are you so hell bent in retrieving treasure which is not ours?"

"Of course, it's the Golden Coracle, it's in disguise," said Kentav as he walked away towards the servant's quarters where Katrin was to lead them out to the orchard.

Ali followed angrily with him as Trent was ahead with Katrin listening.

"I'm not coming to Saundersfoot with you, Kentav. I'm going to New Zealand once I've got back to St. Clears and packed. You're on your own. Whatever is holding you to the Llewellyn's, it's not my problem."

Ali disappeared and left Trent inside with Katrin. Kentav followed in another direction but plain to see from the tree house as Bethesda wrote the pebble for Ivor. The bug dogs followed their leader as Kentav marched briskly towards Saundersfoot, his anger evident. He didn't care about his useless brothers, he'd disown Trent for fraternising with a Llewellyn and Ali, he could defect abroad, as he didn't care. He was going to reclaim all the treasure.

Kentav had been bright. He'd give his dear Blodwen a large brown envelope which had his birth right information. Information that would most certainly bring down the whole of the Llewellyn Empire.

Once he was in one of these castles, which were rightfully his, he would see the infamous Wizard Eddlee Hornblov at the tavern in Cardiff and he would tell all. He couldn't wait to disrupt and discredit the whole of the Llewellyn family, finally.

***

Katrin and Trent sat next to the fake coracle quietly in the dungeon after the two Croggs had left. Trent felt used and was shattered but Katrin was elated as Trent had proposed in a roundabout way and she was thrilled. He would ask her father when he returned. Katrin took his hand, she couldn't wait to wear her special frock that afternoon as there were no parents about and she was going to have some fun at last. She deserved it.

Chapter 22

The Battle preparations.

Again, there was chaos inside the cave. Slobbers and Ivor were being organised by Garibaldi to leave. Hopkin had summoned the coaches and was re- spelling the hovel with Tudor. Elijas and Bedivere were packing as instructed and the animals were listening to Molly.

Harry the horse along with the Ginger twins were planting magical bombs around the cave and half a mile up the beach, to cause some mayhem to the approaching army. By now, they knew that Kentav was leading over a thousand Begglys and they were seriously on route to claim the spoon.

There were several plans afoot and Hopkin waved his triple cuffed cloak towards Molly, and she knew the coaches had arrived. Garibaldi had attached double pins on everyone, Ivor, and Slobbers first as they needed to leave right away.

"Gari, fetch Harry and the twins, we need them on an errand right away, as soon as they've planted all those bombs," commanded Molly after giving Slobbers quiet instructions in his ear. *"Tudor, I want you to go with them as you're a senior wizard."*

258

Tudor looked on in surprise, whatever was she playing at, the enemy were on their way, and she was talking in riddles.

"Ivor, Slobbers, you must leave right away. Hopkin can you see to them. We will see you later. Keep us informed throughout," said Molly waving her tail in the air scattering angel dust over Ivor and Slobbers who looked particularly important.

Before they left, Molly summoned Slobbers to her quarters.

"I have these instructions for you Slobbers. Make friends with Fat Cat and get to the dungeons. You've a link in your chain and once you get close to the coracle, it will start moving and it will try to resist you. You'll need to place your right paw under the ash seat, where there is a hidden box. It's very tiny but your paw will fit. Once you do this the Golden Coracle will glow recognising you as its master. Once you've pawed the coracle, we will come for you. It will not have any powers and if you can drag it outside and wait for us, that would be impressive.

We should be back from this mission by then. I'll expect you to send Gari some crystal pebbles on your progress. Send the feather pebble once you've sight of the coracle. Garibaldi will be making decisions in the cave for us all. Ivor is your decoy, use him."

Hopkin interrupted as they needed to get them away unnoticed. Slobbers left feeling larger than normal, his pride making him appear three times his usual size.

Harry and the ginger twins stuck their heads through the door as Molly continued, no one interrupted as they had little time to debate the next unfolding events.

"Harry, take Tudor and the ginger twins to Llanelli right away. You need to collect weapons from our second cousin immediately. The arms will fill the cart, and Tudor will need to spell them; in order you don't lose any on your return."

"What kind of weapons?" asked Garibaldi a slight unease reaching the pit of his stomach.

"They are pitched arrows encrusted and wrapped in sacking, which means when we set a candle to them, they'll burn immediately. Once thrown they'll instantly kill the Begglys."

Everyone gasped as Molly had been against violence up to now.

"Remember that line everyone. They're here to kill us and find the spoon. There's no time to argue we will defend ourselves and this cave until we're ready to leave. They'll kill us believe me. They've no idea we have the spoon, and we know the whereabouts of the treasure chest, but we must avoid them as much as possible as we would rather have the Croggs to deal with, than the bug dogs. Our mission is to kill the bug dogs tonight and weaken their numbers. This should frighten him off temporarily as he's a coward."

"How?" asked Elijas who hadn't heard of such a stupid idea.

"Harry with the guidance of Tudor will return with another horse and cart as we'll be attacking from two directions. We need to be ready to leave as soon as they return."

Bedivere looked at Garibaldi; they would never pack everything in time.

"It's ok, Gari. We won't be here. We'll spell the cave invisible and leave Yo-Yo with the spoon. At no cost does Yo-Yo leave. However, Yo-Yo, if we fail and you find yourself under attack, you need to get inside the third passageway and get yourself to Tudors' castle immediately. If you administer this secret passageway, the cave will disintegrate. All our belongings will fly to Caernarvon, and we will see the cave flatten in front of our eyes. If this happens, we will have lost the battle and may not be here to see it," said Molly going quiet.

"Where are we going?" said Elijas as everyone started to panic.

"Right, this is what we're going to do. Once we have a status from the hovel, where the enemy are, in around six hours, we will leave. We'll go ahead of them and attack them from behind, they will not be expecting this out-flanking movement; we also call it an encirclement of attack. We shall attack from both sides, and it will force them to retreat as they'll only be looking ahead. This should give us an edge with the element of surprise if we're in the dark. There will be two teams, one each side of the road. Ginger One can throw from Harry's mane as it will give them extra height. The rest of us will be given *a strength dust, just before and our tails should function as a lethal weapon while throwing the pitched arrows.*

Bedivere, you will jump in the second cart once it arrives, along with Ginger Two, Wibbly Alf and me."

Millie looked horrified to be excluded from Wibbly's cart.

"It's okay Millie. Our spells will clash so you need to be with Tudor, Elijas and Ginger One. You will instigate the commencement of fire in your cart," said Molly making Millie aware that she knew of her special powers.

"What about me?" said Garibaldi knowing he had no cart assigned to him.

"Gari, you're head of the family, you must look after Yo-Yo and if anything happens, you must both get to Tudors' or Castell Coch without fail. You need to prepare the cave for demolition, and you've got time to start sending our belongings to Castell Coch in advance of us getting there."

Screeeech.

The hovel started to wail like a thousand kettles as everyone visible jumped.

"Tudor, take Harry and the cats you've got to get back here as soon as you can."

Garibaldi returned red in the face, puffing.

"Their resting outside Manorbier, we've six hours easily."

"Three hours Tudor, as we need to get back and then get ahead of them, before they get to the beach," summarised Molly in full flow.

Tudor left to get Harry and the cats.

The door rattled and the goose walked in before Molly could start on her next bit of instructions. The Huggett spoon started to wriggle from its pouch and the cushion. Yo-Yo jumped on it and realised that this treasure was going to give him more trouble than he'd envisaged but it was the most crucial. He suddenly realised his task was extremely important indeed.

"Yo-Yo, Hopkin will give you some spells for the spoon," said Molly.

Hopkin hadn't been assigned a task and no-one dared ask why as Molly continued to give instructions. Hopkin came back inside as this thought was going through the minds of Elijas especially and he smiled,

"Right, Ivor has been given extra spells Molly. Between them they'll find a way. The three feathers coach Gari is hidden behind the cave, in case you need it, while the others are in battle."

Before Gari could answer there was an almighty crash from the passageways as Geraintus fell into the dining room, again spluttering green dust everywhere.

"Any news?" asked Hopkin sensing something wasn't right as did Molly.

"I'll make some tea," said Garibaldi anxious with worry about Slobbers already.

Geraintus sat at the table, noticing the place appeared packed up and ready. He looked at Molly and around the room as all ears was upon him.

"I've got Robin and Rudge sending messages back to you via the goose. It will be much quicker than me trying to get used to your passageways."

"What's wrong Geraintus?" said Hopkin quietly as Gari rushed back in with Welsh cakes and tea.

"The Croggs are resting at Lydstep, there's over three hundred Begglys, but I've only seen two of the brothers. We're missing one. To date we can't fathom which one is missing but we're still looking. With that in mind it's better for me to be here with Yo-Yo and Garibaldi in case the one brother is acting alone. All the kites in the kingdom are on alert but so far no one has seen sight of one brother."

"What are you going to be doing Hopkin?" asked Elijas who couldn't help himself; he needed to know why the eldest most powerful wizard was not going into battle.

"For your information Elijas and everyone, this is what I'm doing. Once the pink coach returns from dropping Slobbers and Ivor, I will take it and go directly to Castell Coch. There I will negotiate with the Eagles somehow and get the Castle ready for your arrival. When you leave for Castell Coch, you need to be able to fly in with the coach or walk in through the gates. I will have organised a safe route. That's what I'm doing. Any objections?"

Elijas went as red as his cloak and stuffed a Welsh cake in his mouth embarrassed.

"Going back to the Croggs for a minute," said Geraintus impressed with Hopkin as usual, *"The army has stopped three times already, which means we need to be ready to go within three hours, to pass them. The best place to attack them will be around Tenby beach towards New Hedges. We need to kill as many as we can before we land up on this beach otherwise, we will blow ourselves up by our own placed sand bombs. The peninsula of New Hedges beach where there is shelter and the beach is at its widest. One horse and cart will be on the beach, the other on the hedgerow, three gallops behind the beach horse otherwise you're going to attack each other."*

"Will the tide affect us?" asked Molly just realising this fact.

"No, I've already been to see Tom the turtle and he is turning the tide back for the day, all organised."

"Good everyone ok, any questions?" asked Molly swishing round the room sending dust over everyone as they all began to be spelled by her magical aura.

Hopkin departed as the pink coach arrived back safely as Garibaldi checked the hovel. He left and there was silence in the cave as everyone realised that this was the first battle of a few to come and they hoped that they would overcome it and get to Castell Coch as Molly wished.

The Hugglett spoon started to wriggle and Wibbly's link chain started to twinkle in recognition. Millie's turquoise collar started to tingle as everyone sat quiet waiting for Tudor to return with the two horses.

Chapter 23

Magical Molly and the Beggly Army

Time passed terribly slow as Garibaldi and Geraintus prepared the cave. The secret passageways had all been sealed and the hovel enlarged to monitor the movement of the Crogg army. As soon as Tudor returned with Harry the horse and another, they would all leave. They had to get to behind the on-coming army without being noticed.

"They're here," shouted Ginger One as he popped his head inside the cave as he was on watch.

All eyes looked out of the porthole towards the beach and there was Harry and another horse galloping down the beach pulling carts laden of weapons, with Tudor holding Harry's mane for dear life.

"Everyone outside I need to spell you, then we depart. You've all been briefed," instructed Molly as the animals moved out prepared for battle.

"Vamos muchachos," shouted Molly swirling her tail in the air and cascading angel dust on everyone. All the animals jumped into their designated cart.

"See you in Castell Coch," grinned Hopkin. *"I'll send a coach party if I don't see you in three days."*

He looked straight at Tudor, Elijas and Bedivere with a warning look as all three wizards acknowledged its meaning.

"I shall follow you Molly," shouted Tudor from the other cart, trying to get his breath back from the ride on Harry. *"Which direction are we headed?"*

"New Hedges and we need to move fast. We need to circle around and get behind them before they twig, there's no one here, apart from Garibaldi and Geraintus. Yo-Yo keep the spoon safe, get inside. Everyone, the magical green candle wax in the black cloths is to be used to set fire to the spears and arrows, ok? Right, let's go."

Off they cantered as Molly realised that she may not see one or two of her family ever again.... She ignored this thought and concentrated in moving the horse and cart as fast as they could towards New Hedges to encircle the enemy.

***

Hopkin Paulinus left a very sombre Giant and fidgety dwarf in the cave as he swirled off in his pink cape with little crests and moons on it. The pink coach leapt to attention and as he ascended, the glass steps disappeared. The coach left a tell-tale pink cloud for a moment as it disappeared from the hovel's tracking and Garibaldi went to make more tea. Geraintus sat making notes on the whispering fig tree plan of attack, as Yo-Yo was huddled inside his jacket for extra protection, the spoon attached to his tummy for safety too.

***

Ivor and Slobbers had arrived at Llawhaden Castle and had worked out a plan of attack. It would all depend on how Thomas Beckett received Ivor. They would decide how they were going to inspect the dungeons after their initial reception. Slobbers was going to act dim and see what would happen with fat cat. He was also feeling important as Molly had given him incredibly exclusive information and he was to oversee calming the coracle with his fat paw.

They sat on the wall outside the castle as Slobbers began thinking, what if the coracle wasn't even there. Goodness he mustn't think such terrible thoughts. They sat on the wall as the pink coach had thrown them out, wanting to fly back in haste to fetch their master Hopkin. At least the three feathers coach was hovering behind the big oak tree in the distance and Slobbers felt slightly reassured of this fact.

***

Harry and his companion galloped as fast as they could with the load of arrows and animals on their carts. Molly was in deep thought and giving out spells to her team. Millie was doing the same in the other cart, concentrating hard as the mere fact she might lose Wibbly that evening was affecting her spell. She realised at that moment how special he'd become.

The pitched arrows were light to manage and once lit they should be able to kill a few Begglys she hoped; before they realised, they were under attack.

***

Ali was annoyed with his brother and even more annoyed that he was marching towards Saundersfoot and about to confront the Llewellyn wizards about a spoon. Ali knew it didn't belong to them, so why was Kentav besotted about it? It didn't make sense at all. He ran to catch up with him as Kentav looking bedraggled and dishevelled totally focused on marching towards the beach.

"Kentav slow down, for goodness' sake. Don't you think you should think this through, before demanding where the spoon is? It's not even ours. You know this. What wrong with you?"

"I thought you were off to New Zealand," said a sarcastic Kentav.

"I can't let you do this on your own. There's obviously something I don't understand, but I am still loyal even though you've lied to me and Trent," said Ali catching up with him properly and marching at the same pace. *"Look Kentav, what are you trying to achieve? The wizards are decrepit and old but they're still wizards and still have amazing powers, we can't avoid this fact; therefore, marching to their cave is purely stupid and risky."*

"I want the spoon, and I want to be lord of the kingdom Ali, it's important to me. The treasure is ours; I only need the spoon to prove it," said Kentav not convincing Ali one bit.

"Kentav, the crest isn't ours. We don't have a candle in the tapestry. When I saw the Llewellyn's go off with

Owain, this proved to me that our crest was not the same, as you've claimed. The treasure was never ours, was it?"

Kentav hurried his pace and looked towards the ground avoiding Ali's eye contact for a moment, which confirmed to Ali that he was right.

"I've had a problem with the Llewellyn's all my life Ali. The Begglys are programmed to kill them; we're going to be heads of these castles. It's too late to reconsider."

Kentav held back, did he want to inform Ali, what was in the envelope that he'd given his wife for safe keeping? He should just come clean and tell him. Ali interrupted his thoughts.

"Ok, we take the spoon then what?"

"Once we take the spoon, we'll declare to Owain Glyndwr, that we're the rightful owners, it's simple," said Kentav.

Ali wasn't so sure, as they marched together towards Saundersfoot as brothers. But Ali didn't feel like Kentav's brother at all.

***

The two carts sped swiftly and silently through the evening twilight on side roads near the beach head towards New Hedges. Harry's mate Henry was equally fast and both carts moved together until Molly gave the signal to split up. Garibaldi, in the cave was observing. Molly looked at her team and they all nodded back at her, all knowing this was crucial to get right. The road was getting narrower, and the signal would soon arrive from Garibaldi.

In the meantime, Garibaldi was preparing the pebble to send via goose and Geraintus was planting extra coal bombs around the circumference of the cave. Coal bombs had already been placed three miles either side of the cave on the beach in various points, but Geraintus decided they needed more.

The pebble arrived on Molly's cart as the road seemed to disappear; the accuracy of the hovel map was reassuring. Molly moved their cart gently down towards the beach head and turned round. The others were above on the hedge itself and a few feet ahead, already turned around not to clash with them. Ahead of them, they could see the glimmer oval shape of the Begglys marching on the beach with two Croggs at the front of them. They looked like a sea of black heads moving like ants towards an object. Molly knew this object was Ivor's cave.

Bedivere looked worried as did Elijas but as Molly looked at all her team, she swished her tail in the air quietly prayed for her family and repeated three times,

"Niagra Belleeck, encarna lerin..."

Both Harry and Henry started to trot at a reasonable pace towards the back of the moving army as the arrows started to fly from both carts. The arrows were lit by the green candle aura and each one flew alight and hit each Beggly with great accuracy, burning them to death. Ginger Two had a system and was throwing arrows with great aim. Bedivere with one eye on the sand banks and the other passing the lighted arrows to the cat was thoroughly enjoying himself and had not missed one Beggly target yet. The arrows coming from the top cart were also accurate with their aim as tens of Begglys laid on the sand disintegrating and burning up.

"Let's hope the Croggs don't turn round just yet," shouted Wibbly.

As he spoke the leader Bug dog, Zupp turned round and stood facing the oncoming cart,

"Don't stop. Kill him," shouted Molly at Wibbly who didn't hesitate threw a double lighted arrow right at the leader. Zupp's antennae was swirling round as Wibbly threw the arrow at him. As this clashed, Bedivere noticed Begglys crawling up the sand banks and sent Millie a message, praying she could deal with it. They were under attack.

Zupp's live antennae hit the lighted arrow, and the arrow fell back onto the cart as Molly screamed,

"Off the cart, it's going to blow......."

The explosion was horrific and there was no time to think about anyone as they all got thrown in the air, the remaining lighted arrows exploding inside the cart. Henry unhinged himself from the burning cart and fled down the beach as the wizards and animals rolled away from the fire, the smoke thick as soot.

"They've been hit," shouted Millie from the other cart. *"We must help them."*

"No one's leaving the cart, we must get to Kentav and Ali and attack them, follow our orders," shouted Tudor whose aim was particularly accurate to his utter surprise.

"To your left," shouted Ginger One, *"They've seen us. Quick we must get rid of some more before Kentav challenges us."*

"Millie, aim at the Croggs, they're within distance, quick. Send the double lighted ones, now," shouted Bedivere.

Elijas and Millie continued to throw arrows and before Kentav realised what had happened, two spears hit his tall Welsh hat, which annoyed him tremendously. He turned full circle and realised three quarters of his bug dogs were dead and scattered on the beach. He quickly ordered the remaining bug dogs to retreat. The bug dogs turned and disappeared over the cliff ahead of the cart and the two Croggs disappeared with them as quickly as they'd arrived.

"Quick, let's go and find the others," shouted Tudor, who had been impressed with Elijas' throwing skills. *"Harry, take us down to the beach."*

Bedivere was on the beach, checking the dead bugs and had dug a hole and had left Molly, severely burnt with his cloak over her. He was looking for Wibbly Alf and Ginger Two. The others soon helped.

"Over here," shouted Tudor.

Wibbly Alf and Ginger Two were sprawled on the sand, lifeless.

"They're alive just, Harry bring the cart quick."

Bedivere carried Molly to the cart as the others placed both cat and dog inside.

"We shouldn't canter down the beach with the animals so badly injured, Bedivere, shall we summon the three feathers coach, it will be quicker?"

"Do it," said Bedivere as he examined the animals as they looked close to death. *"I thought the three feathers coach was hanging around Ivor and Slobbers, in case they needed to make a quick get away?"* said Elijas not really understanding these wizard's logic at all.

"Yes, but this is urgent. The Begglys may come back any minute, just because we can't see them right now, they could be lying in wait further down. We need the coach," said Bedivere as he nodded to Millie, who set about her spell right away,

"Gorgosgorgos gwych/ghorgosghorgos guweech," as she repeated three times swishing her tail as taught by Molly.

The three feathers coach arrived in two seconds perplexed at being summoned to the beach but landed with dignity near the cart.

"Baja Solana Cochwyn nawr/Bahjah Solanah kochween nahur," instructed Millie as the double glass doors opened to full capacity as the horse and cart with everyone around it rose in the air and disappeared

inside. The doors slammed shut and the coach swirled like a tornado and landed in the secret passageway of Ivor's cave in seconds, as Tudor and Bedivere started on their soothing and healing spells.

Elijas watched on and realised that Molly, Wibbly Alf and Ginger Two were barely alive, who was going to rescue Ivor and Slobbers at Llawhaden Castle?

Of course, they may not need to be rescued but they had no coach to help them right now, which was a concern.

They were short of help in every direction. How were they going to sort this mess out before the Croggs of St. Clears returned with a strengthened army. And what about Ivor, he was certainly harbouring secrets, he was sure of it. Elijas sighed; he'd got involved with an incompetent family.

And Hopkin had disappeared with some pretext about securing that Castle, he was a bit miffed about that. This didn't seem right either. They were not all as one. He could sense it. Mind you they didn't know what he knew either, decent job really as then he might be banned from being Bedivere's friend if they knew the whole truth. He knew why Ivor was holding back....

***

Kentav Crogg was furious at the family, even more so than earlier. How dare they attack him from behind. He would return even stronger; he didn't need his weak brothers . He would show them. He knew things that no-one else knew and he was going to expose them all, once he was King of all the Castles.

***

Garibaldi looked on in horror as the injured animals were rushed into the cave. They needed Molly and all of them fit for a rescue at Llawhaden Castle. He knew that Ivor was not going to cope, once he realised the glass coach had disappeared which was his back up plan.

Was this treasure hunt worth it and why wasn't Ivor willing to come clean and tell them? He had secrets even he may not be aware of. He shuddered, he truly hoped not.

That was impossible, or was it? Surely Ivor Ap Llewellyn didn't have more secrets that the ones he already knew of.

Gary baulked at the very thought of more secrets than he knew.

What he knew was enough.......

Kentav Crogg

www.ingramcontent.com/pod-product-compliance
Lightning Source LLC
Chambersburg PA
CBHW071428200726
48294CB00002B/558